Blood and Electricity

For Rebecca

Blood and Electricity

Steven John

With Friendship

Steve

Bridge House

British Library Cataloguing in Publication Data
A Record of this Publication is available from the British
Library

ISBN 978-1-914199-80-6

This edition published 2024 by Bridge House Publishing
Manchester, England

Contents

Foreword

I first read two short stories by a writer new to me, Steven John, in early 2016. He submitted them to Stroud Short Stories, the twice-yearly live literary event I ran then and still run for writers based in Gloucestershire. They didn't make the final cut.

The next story he submitted, 'Sculpted Bones', a story about a relationship, set on a tour of rural Wales, walked into the Final Ten for the next event and he performed it on stage, rather nervously, at 'The Apocalypse Alphabet and Other Stories' in November 2016. It's a haunting story of emotional emptiness amid the materialism and mundanity of life – and is in this collection.

Since then, no one has performed more times at Stroud Short Stories events than Steven, and he has grown into a consummate performer enjoying an intimate relationship with large audiences.

I have been able, with Steven's permission, to publish his works in two Stroud Short Stories anthologies, both local best sellers. All those stories are in this collection.

Indeed, one of my favourites of Steven's stories, 'Puffballs', I selected as one of the seven stories at the 'Stroud Short Stories Greatest Hits' event at Cheltenham Literature Festival in October 2022. I could equally have chosen another of my favourites, 'The Orange Tree' after which we named our event in May 2022. Or 'Burning the Stubble', from 'Incendiary!', our May 2019 event, which opens this collection.

Steven hasn't just stayed local of course. He has been published scores of times in online and printed literary journals across the world; has won international prizes for his short stories and flash fiction; been Senior Fiction Editor of New Flash Fiction Review and co-founded the online literary magazine *The Phare*. It says much of Steven that he continues to submit to and perform at a community event like Stroud Short Stories.

These days, as well as writing, Steven loves teaching and critiquing creative writing, something he does for the University of Gloucestershire and for creative writing groups based locally. Nothing pleases him more than the success of his students.

There are stories in this collection that relate to Steven's early years in the West Midlands. There is one story that takes us to Canada. But mainly these are stories about individuals and their relationships, or about tensions within families or social groups.

Steven's stories are never tricksy or fashionable. The stories here are mostly quiet, the landscape or physical environment he creates mirroring the feelings of the characters. His concern is for the human condition, to convey feelings rather than portray action.

Certainly his characters, sometimes isolated, or even invisible, may feel either disappointment or joy. But they are more often on a knife-edge between these emotions. Sometimes the stories resolve this tension and sometimes they do not. (A character in 'The Composer's Tall Trees' is described at the end as 'almost hopeful'.) As readers, we share the characters' fears and hopes, and recognise their vulnerabilities in ourselves. Overall, I would say that we understand ourselves better for reading his stories.

This is Steven's first collection of short stories. We can inevitably look forward to more.

John Holland
Organiser/Editor, Stroud Short Stories
May 2024

Burning the Stubble

We both go down on one knee in the perimeter of the field that grills under the August sun. You take an oily rag from your trouser pocket and, in a single jerk, tear it in two. You press both halves of the rag into the inch of tractor diesel I've carried from the barn in an empty paint tin. Whilst the rags soak, you stand and slide a cigarette from behind your ear. I stand with you, take a lighter from my pocket, offer up a tooth of flame. You draw in deep lungfuls then exhale slowly upwards into the baked air. The blue smoke drifts over the velvet of cut straw. You're feeling the wind direction on your face, watching the path of cigarette smoke. We've ploughed a firebreak on the east side.

By the time the flames reach the break they'll be at a gallop, white hot, licking out twelve feet horizontal to the ground like a stampede of dragons. Without the break, the east hedge would be charred sticks in the time it takes to fry a rasher of bacon. You flick-arc your cigarette end into the stubble and nod. I pull the rags from the diesel, ball them up, spear them onto our pitchforks and light them. When our hands feel the heat we stride off in opposite directions, trailing a riptide of fire that submerses everything.

With the tsunami of flame already half a furlong down, we meet back in the middle. I look up at two giant white birds converging on the mirage of heat.

'Glider pilots scan the sky for smoke,' you say. 'Flying into it pushes them up a thousand feet. Like taking a lift to the top floor.'

Of course, you've done that. Flown a glider. There's nothing you haven't done. You've told me the stories.

Skied in the Arctic Circle with your snot turned to ice, ballooned over pyramids drunk on champagne, sailed a yacht across the channel, basked in the winner's enclosure with your own racehorse.

'He's not a bloody farmer, he's a playboy,' my father said when I told him I'd got a summer job on your farm. 'He won't teach you anything about the land. Drinking beer and chasing skirt more like,' he says.

It's true you're not like any other farmer in the village. You demolished the old farmhouse and built an upside-down bachelor pad in its place; king-size waterbeds downstairs and floor to ceiling smoked glass east and west, upstairs. You say the rising and setting sun is the only clock a man needs.

Back at what you still call the farmhouse, you open beers and climb the open staircase to turn on the sauna. You strip naked. Drop your smoky clothes on the carpet for the Filipino maid to launder. The crack of your arse spreads itself over the burgundy leather of your armchair. Apart from the leather suite, a television and the retro magazine rack over-stuffed with your horse-racing newspapers, there's no other furniture.

I open sliding doors onto the balcony that overlooks your acres. The smoke from the torched field rises like a tornado into the early evening sky, funnelling into the amber clouds. I watch the black flecks of burnt, glowing straw massing like a swarm of fireflies, spiralling up the vortex of heat.

'Why don't you phone home and tell them that you're staying here tonight?' you call out. 'We have to be up early tomorrow to burn the others. Rain forecast day after.'

I can hear horse racing commentary from the television. When the little red light goes out on the sauna's thermostat, you'll expect me to strip off and join you. I didn't like being naked in the school changing rooms with boys my own age. I'm the type who puts my shirt on before pulling off my trunks. I re-enter the sitting room and pick the telephone off the floor.

'I'm staying at Dave's tonight. We have to be up early tomorrow… YES, it's alright, he asked me to.'

'She worries now Dad's gone,' I say.

You open more beers and take yours towards the sauna room. 'You need plenty of fluid inside you to sweat back out.'

I take off my clothes and put my jeans up to my nose, remember bonfires with my Dad. That was my job whilst he trimmed the hedges. I fold my clothes neatly on the sofa.

You're hunched over a Dick Francis paperback in your usual spot by the burner. I step up to the higher level and lie on my back. When the sweat starts to run you'll begin scraping your hands over your groin, flicking the wet onto the glowing coals. I'll lie here listening to the spit and hiss.

After cool showers and more beer, you drive us at reckless speed through the country lanes in your open topped car. The smoke from the field is all around us. Other cars have their headlights on. My mother will have taken the washing in, closed the bedroom windows, even locked the doors with me not coming home.

'Farmers burning every damn thing in sight again,' is what she says.

We arrive at the pub you part own. You order us rare steaks and red wine.

'You've done a good job today,' you say.

It doesn't feel like I've done anything apart from light rags and fags. You know everyone. Everyone wants to know you. I feel the reflected glory. You take the piss out of the lads at the bar.

'Propping up the bar all day, have we? Make room for the workers,' you say. They lap it up.

'Dave's in. Dave's buying. He's the man'

'Are you going to the races tomorrow, Dave?'

'Got any winners for us losers, Dave?'

You let me drive home. You say I haven't got a license to lose.

Above the balcony, bats flit through the smoke of the joint we pass between us. A fox yelps in the spinney, hunts its prey. A breeze ripples embered lines over the ashen field, forks of red lightning flattened into the soil, shallow orange wavelets lapping over footprints.

We drink whisky until the carpet starts to sway. I'm in an armchair boat on a choppy sea. I can see your lips moving but can't hear. I wake when I feel your rough hands under the duvet, exploring me. You're naked again, kneeling next to the bed you dropped me into. You look down at what you want me to see.

At dawn, from the balcony, I see the black heart of the land. Wisps of smoke rise ghostlike from six feet under, meld with the mist that sulks in the ditches. The fertile soil is scorched, cremated, rendered down for a different crop.

A Brief History of Time in Our House

This second is the same as the last, a press of the screen, the same exhalation. We lie in bed, scrolling social intercourse. Our hearts have pumped eight ounces of blood.

Minutes replicate themselves like bacteria. Your quantum of likes leaves you unloved. We have breathed three and a half gallons of air.

Little is different in this hour. Our livers have metabolised another drink, the sky sticks on black with white moon. Lunar and menstrual cycles are looping. With variant ingredients we cook the same suppers. Together we have shed a complete layer of skin.

We took an excursion around the sun again this year, five hundred million miles back to where we started. The Earth is a fraction warmer although it doesn't feel it here. We expended another 1.25% of our lives, give or take.

On the event horizon of a black hole, time is white. Our white blood cells die every day.

Chameleons

In the windless sky a pink cloud floats over the chameleon in the sycamore tree. A giant green chameleon, with its back arched over the tree's crown, its triangular head reaching down for a tongue-flick at its prey, its spiny tail counter-balancing down the leafy branches. Strange what you see when you sit in a chair and look out of a window long enough. The pink cloud is real though, for now at least. Annie reads the text from her lover for the tenth time.

'CRITICAL we stop seeing each other.'

Annie hears her husband leave his bedroom, walk along the landing into the bathroom and bolt the door. She hears her son Fin coughing in his attic bedroom above. Hay fever he'll tell her. More likely the effect of the weed he smokes leaning out of his bedroom window. They see each other at night when she wafts outside for a cigarette. Fin looks down and sees his mum take wine and a lighter around the back. Puffs of different flavoured smoke clouding into the night sky. Indoors, in their mother/son lives, they make believe they don't smoke. They homogenise with their non-smoking husband/father.

Annie's lover has confessed to his wife. His wife moved her clothes into a spare bedroom then threatened to leave him, but Annie's husband didn't need to be told. He said he could smell it. The affair. But that doesn't matter. They're history anyway. Annie and her lover had made plans to go house-hunting, make a weekend of it. They were going to start a new life together. Annie's lover sends another text.

'Can't do this to her. She's been good to me'

Fin is taking a critical exam today. University or not. Pivotal. He hasn't done any revision. Piles of untidy, scribbled notes on his bedroom floor. The revision timetable Annie put together, ignored. Fin's teachers predict the worst. She's heard him strumming his guitar, listening to music, watching porn on his phone probably. Anything except learn. But the three of them exist under the same roof, keep up the charade. They continue to talk about university options. *'That's what we do in this house,'* thinks Annie, *'clothe ourselves in background colours.'*

Annie's lover was her first since being married, first in over twenty years, first time she'd had sex in five. They met at night-school, local college, Organic Gardening. An after-class drink in a pub. Sandwiches together in town during their lunch-hours. A furtive weekend away under the pretext of a class field trip. Cosy rented cottage, lunch in a country inn, strolling hand in hand around a stately home garden. Indistinguishable from other couples in the tearoom. On her phone, she has a single photograph of them together. They asked a gardener to take it in the grounds of the stately home. They spoke to him about azaleas. He told them how the flowering shrub needs perfect conditions to survive. Annie and her lover have exchanged hundreds of online messages, texts, emails. An electronic courtship. Virtual love. Grown organically, from nothing, no noxious chemicals.

Annie dresses and goes downstairs, makes coffee, sets the breakfast table for two. Her husband hasn't eaten breakfast since the silence began. He doesn't eat any meal with her. He walks through the kitchen to the utility room, polishes his office shoes. The kitchen is silent apart from the hiss of the kettle and thrum of the fridge. She hears Fin bolt the bathroom door, the buzz of the electric shower.

Annie takes her coffee back to her single bedroom. She tells people she's in between jobs. Having a break. That's what people say when they don't want a fuss. The grass needs mowing. Perhaps she'll do it after the dew has risen. There's a deer in the garden eating the heads off her husband's roses. Annie would normally have taken a photo of the deer and texted it to her lover. Annie's left hand trembles in the morning. Her GP told her there's nothing to worry about.

'Drink decaf,' he said.

This morning her hand trembles more than usual. She feels breathless, as though someone is holding her tightly around the chest. She paces up and down her room. She starts a text back to her lover.

'I'm destroyed,' but doesn't send.

Nothing is said at the breakfast table. Fin eats his cereal and plays a game on his phone. She smears her toast with low-fat spread and watches it melt. Before he leaves for work her husband goes through his pockets, finds lunch money for their teenager. He asks Fin if he's got everything for his exam. Pen, calculator, notes to revise in his breaks. Fin says yes. They all know he hasn't made any notes. '*That's how it's always been*,' Annie thinks. '*We camouflage facts, say things that fit.*'

Fin is dressed to blend in: jeans, odd socks, Bob Marley t-shirt, filthy trainers. She finds her car keys to give him a lift.

'Okay?' she asks Fin.

'Okay.'

'Is it okay to sit an exam in filthy trainers?'

'It's fine.'

'He's typical,' people have assured her. 'He's no different.'

Last week, in the car, on the way home from school, Annie told her son about the situation.

'Things aren't great,' she said.

'Okay,' he said.

'We haven't been getting on for some time.'

'It's fine.'

16

'You must've noticed.'

'Sometimes.'

'That's how things are sometimes,' she said.

When they're in the car together, Annie and Fin, they listen to music. Which station depends which one of them turns on the radio first. They dislike each other's choice. This morning neither of them turns on the radio.

'Given any more thought to uni?' she asks.

'Not really.'

She doesn't want to think about what happens next either. She'd rather nothing has changed or will change. She wants to think about her lover and what she can do to keep them together. Annie thinks about her lover in bed with her, on their weekend away, after sex when he'd said, 'I feel sad.'

She'd quizzed him on why.

'I don't know. I wish I did,' he said.

'You must know something,' she'd said, over and over.

'I wish I hadn't told you.'

As Annie and Fin drive through the lanes, a buzzard flies in front of them, flies low, barely high enough for them to pass beneath. There's a baby rabbit in its talons, its back legs thrusting into thin air. She can hear it squealing.

'Did you see that?' Annie asks.

'What?'

The buzzard with a baby rabbit. I swear I could hear it crying.'

'No. You're seeing things.'

She and Fin stay silent until she pulls up outside school. Fin gets out.

'Do your best, darling, okay,' she says.

'Will do,' he says, but Annie's weeping, not listening. She's not seeing things. She pecks out a text.

'CRITICAL we don't.'

17

Holly's Party

I haven't seen you for months. The last time was your twenty-first birthday. I felt like a ghost gate-crashing a party for the living, and my God, were you living. The partying never ended for you that summer.

At the door of the restaurant a waitress greeted me as though I'd come to inspect the food hygiene. You'd told me it was a 'club' not a restaurant.

'Restaurants are for dead people,' you said.

I gave the waitress my jacket. She held it as though it was contaminated and looked around as if someone might help. I took it back and told her not to worry.

'I'm with my daughter Holly's party,' I said.

She led me to your table. I felt invisible. The high-pitched laughter and clang of beer bottles. You'd told me before to not say things like 'what happened to drinking from glasses?' You said it made me sound like an old fart. I was determined not to say anything old fart-ish.

'Benjamin!' you screamed. ('I'm not calling you 'Daddy' now I'm twenty-one,' you'd said.)

'Everybody, say hello to Benjamin!' Beer bottles raised and clinked. I tried laughing, but it came out as a cough.

'Twenty-one years ago, Benjamin had something to do with me being here,' you shouted.

Your friends jeered and I felt my face redden. Like being called out for an illicit sex act with your mother. Your mother would have been better at all this. I would have stood behind her and smiled, and paid the bill, and called the taxis, and felt I'd played my small part well enough. Now I have to play one of the lead roles, but can't learn the lines.

I sat down next to you. You introduced me to people whose names I instantly forgot.

18

'Benjamin, you have to start with a Stinger,' you said and waved at the waitress.

I must have looked at you in that way you say is 'demented'.

'Russian vodka with a drizzle of bitters. Keep up, Benjamin,' you said.

'We called it Pink Gin,' I said, 'although it had gin, not vodka.' I'd said something old fart-ish already.

'We've ordered sliders for everyone,' you said, or was it slippers, I can't remember. Small hamburgers, but I didn't feel I could say that.

I tried to talk to you about you mother. How she would have loved this moment. How much she would have loved your boyfriend, but I must remember to say partner. But you didn't want to talk about your mother.

'Lighten up, Benjamin,' you said.

I drank too much. I couldn't keep up with all the conversations. Too many voices and my ears can't cope. I watched you be like your mother was when she was twenty-one. The centre of everything. But she had always held my hand under the table. I held on to my jacket on my lap.

You followed me out of the restaurant to my taxi. We hugged each other and your thin body shook with sobs. You held me so tight.

'Come home with me, Holly,' I said. 'You don't have to move in with him. Take a few days to decide.'

'No, I'm fine, Daddy,' you said, 'really, I'm fine.'

The Orange Tree

The Portuguese sun volleyed onto the white walls of their rented villa and ricocheted around them; through the chemical blue water of the swimming-pool, over the towel-covered loungers and into the marble-floored sitting room. It burnt their English noses and cooked the hire-car on the road outside. Behind the bedroom's wooden shutters, Philip could hear the ceaseless chatter of his wife Joanna and their two young children in the pool. He couldn't sleep any longer.

Philip had been up with the kids since before dawn. Playing snap, doing a puzzle they'd found in a cupboard, and watching cartoons on T.V. in Portuguese. The children were still buzzing since arriving at the villa late the previous night. They'd been delayed at Heathrow for seven hours. Joanna had bought them a battery-operated toy dog that barked, walked, then did a backwards flip. After four hours in the departure lounge, Philip had flipped.

'Stuff the holiday. It's only a week. By the time we get there it'll be time to come home,' he said.

'And waste a thousand pounds? To do what exactly?' Joanna asked. 'Let me guess. You escape back to work while I sit with the children, watch the rain come down, and go mad.'

They'd rowed in the airport terminal. They hadn't spoken during the flight or during the two-hour drive to the villa. The children were used to the long silences and had learnt to keep quiet.

Joanna was still hungover from the complimentary bottles of white and red wine that had been left by the villa company. They'd opened them after putting the children to bed, promised each other to make the best of it for the kids' sake, then somehow sex had happened on the rug in front of the fireplace with fake logs. Philip had reached over her head and turned on the toy dog. It had been a long time since they'd laughed during sex.

When the sun was still low, after giving the children their cereal, Philip told them to go and wake their mother.

'She'll know where to find your swimming stuff,' he said.

Joanna appeared outside by the pool, still in her pyjamas. He was sitting on a lounger, looking at his phone.

'Thanks for arranging the wake up,' she said.

'My turn for a lie-in now.'

'Since when has seven thirty in the morning been a lie-in?'

'Since 5am, when I got up with them.'

Now, Philip went outside holding a beer.

'Here's Daddy,' said Joanna. 'He can dive in with you while I make a well-deserved coffee.'

'After I've finished this drink, I'm going shopping,' he said.

'They've been waiting for you.'

'And what are we going to eat, exactly?'

'Can't it wait for an hour?' Joanna said.

'I did enough waiting yesterday. In an hour it will be too hot to go shopping.'

The hire car was in the shade of a tree that stood in a patch of dry scrub on the other side of a white-washed wall. The wall divided their villa from the square of deserted grove that awaited the foundations of yet another new villa. Philip looked up into the tree as he unloaded the last few bags from their late arrival. The branches were laden with oranges, under-ripe and green. Where the sun pierced through the

21

thick canopy of dark green leaves, some were beginning to show signs of ripening, like dawn breaking on their smooth skins. It would be weeks before they were ready. Joanna came out to the car wrapped in a towel.

'Pick up something for a picnic lunch. We'll go to the beach when you get back.'

'Can't we stay around the pool? We've paid for it.'

'They need a change. Try and enjoy yourself. We've paid for all of it.'

Philip watched his wife and kids paddling in the shallows and jumping the waves as they petered out over the hot sand. Further out, the Atlantic swell was deep blue and heavy. A few adults and teenagers had hired the yellow, open-decked canoes and surfed in, steering the craft across the face of the waves, like flying fish, cutting and slicing. He walked over to the dread-locked man who sat on a deckchair under a bleached-white sun umbrella. The man's chair was surrounded by canoes and piles of old life-vests that looked past their best. Philip had watched the man amble to the sea with a child's bucket, fill it with seawater, then walk back to his dog that lay in the shade of the umbrella, and slowly pour the water over its back.

'I've hired a canoe and a child's life-vest for an hour. I'll take the kids out, one at a time,' Philip said to his wife.

'They're a bit young, aren't they? Have you seen the size of those breakers?

'It's perfectly safe. These canoes are made for beginners, which I'm not.' Philip called his daughter over and strapped her into the life-vest.

His wife and son watched from the sea edge as he paddled out over the breakers to the deeper water. He turned the canoe and, looking over his shoulder, picked out

22

the swell they'd ride. His daughter was the braver child of the two. From her front seat, she laughed and waved at her mother and brother as the canoe rose and fell on the humps. Then the one he'd chosen arrived. He paddled fast to move the canoe up to the same speed as the rising blue wall, then they were on it, high above the trough. He dug in on his left and accelerated with the water as it charged towards the beach. Then he dug in on his right, the bows swung around and zig-zagged the boat back the other way. Moments before the wave broke, he straightened up and surfed in, with the cold white foam cascading over their shoulders. He unloaded the laughing child into her mother's arms.

'I spent whole summers doing this,' he said. 'Try and enjoy yourself. We've paid for all of it.'

'He's younger, remember,' she said and strapped their son into the life-vest.

By the time Philip reached the deeper water and turned the canoe stern on to the swell, the boy asked to go back.

'Just one ride in, ok?' said Philip. 'Just one.'

Philip turned the canoe right and left on the wave as he had before, but the boy was crying. He straightened out as the wave broke, but the angle was too steep. The bows pierced into the swirling water and headed for the bottom. The hump of water at the stern, upended the canoe and cartwheeled it over. Philip was thrown into the churning blue and white interior of the wave. His vision was a blur of bubbles and sand, rising in the suck of water. He didn't know which way was up. Then his feet found solid ground.

His head came out of the water to see Joanna wading in as fast as she was able, already waist deep. She was bellowing something at him, but he couldn't decipher her words. He saw the capsized canoe a few yards in front but couldn't see their boy. Philip thrashed to the boat, stood, and righted it. The boy's head was in the air-pocket, trapped but floating.

Without a word, Joanna snatched her child from Philip's arms and headed for the shore. Philip walked the canoe back to the sand and dragged it to the man in the chair. By the time he returned to his family, Joanna had packed everything up. The boy was wrapped in a towel, shivering.

'He's okay, just a bit shaken. He says he wants to go back and play in the pool,' she said.

'Sure, we'll go back. Shall we stop and buy you that inflatable shark you saw yesterday?' he said to the boy.

'Will you come in the pool with us, Daddy?' the boy asked.

'Sure, I'll come in the pool with you. We'll both go in the pool with him, won't we Mummy?'

Early the next morning, before the sun was fully up and before the children had woken, Philip drove to the marketplace where the food sellers were setting up their stalls. He bought a large box of fresh, ripe oranges. When he returned to the villa, he placed a dozen fruit under the orange tree, then set up a breakfast table by the pool.

'Wouldn't it be wonderful to squeeze some fresh orange juice for our breakfast,' he said to the children when they appeared, still in their pyjamas. 'Why don't you take a look under the orange tree? Take your beach buckets.' He listened to their excited screams as they collected the orange treasure from the shade beneath the tree.

Philip put oranges under the tree at dawn every morning for the remaining five days. Every morning the family ate breakfast together and squeezed oranges, while the ripe sun rose and bled something sweet into their lives.

Bluebells, Cockle Shells

After the men lay the smooth tarmac road, new games began on the estate. The best game was roller-skiing. Boys on their bikes, a length of rope attached to their saddles, towed along the girls on roller-skates, hanging on to a cricket stump like water-skiers. Faster, faster, faster till our hair whips our ears, till eyes streamed wind-tears down our cheeks, till our school skirts press tight into our nonnies. There were no brakes. The pansies chickened out, let go of the stump and rumbled into the grass verge. Us tomboys went so fast we felt sick, hit a drain cover and slashed our knees through ripped tights. The bravest roller-skiers make jumps consisting of planks ramped up on bricks. We flew over the younger kids or landed on their chubby legs and yelled into their faces, 'Next time, it'll be your little willy.'

The girls who weren't tomboys lined up their bare knees on the front garden walls, hiked up their skirts and twiddled their hair along with the bloodshed. Others span washing-lines through the air while first one girl skipped, then two, then three, until someone mucked up, and they'd sing:

'Bluebells, cockle shells
Eevie, Ivy, Over
I like coffee, I like tea
I like the boys and the boys like me'

When the skates were all played out, there was the recreation ground. Down an alleyway of dandelions and dog shit, we chewed gum and smoked chocolate cigarettes on the merry-go-round. The boys carried weapons; spud guns, catapults and sometimes a box of matches and sixpenny bangers. While us girls were on the swings, the boys climbed the frames and looked up our skirts. We played kiss-chase through the play-tunnels, and when the boys caught us, we snogged them. Sarah Colman showed Alan Nesbitt her knickers and showed Michael Newman a whole lot more.

Then we'd go to Maddy's house whose mum made raspberry lemonade, and we'd go to Maddy's bedroom, sit on her bed and pick at each other's scabs. We'd guess which boys fancied us, except for Lulu who everyone knew was adopted. No-one fancied Lulu except for Maddy's dad, who came into the bedroom, put his face up close to her and said she was his little flower.

Sea Loch

We found the cottage eventually. It was in a row of other dirty-white fisherman's dwellings at the head of the grey sea-loch. 'Dramatic Highland Views' was what the brochure said, and there were some, albeit fleetingly, when the Scottish mist lifted its woollen skirts off the surrounding mountains, and the relentless rain regrouped.

We pulled on coats and boots, walked across the deserted single-track road onto the shingle beach. You picked coloured stones and shells from under the seaweed and cosseted them in your coat pocket. I turned over dead jellyfish with the toe of my boot.

'What are you collecting those for?' I asked.

'I'll do something when we get home,' you said.

I bent down and picked you a heart shaped piece of something sea-smooth. You turned it over in your fingers and dropped it.

'Only glass,' you said.

We walked from one end of the beach to the other and back again. When you weren't picking things up, I held your hand. And in the brief moments when the sun shone, I lifted your ring-finger up to the rays, tried to prism the whiteness through the single diamond. We did it a hundred times but never got the deep blues they'd shown us under the jeweller's desk light.

After two days you said the rain was stretching the limits of your endurance, as though we were crossing a sea in an inflatable dingy. The double bed was damp and the mattress concave and shot. You said it was too high off the ground. Draughty. There was a yellow stained chamber pot with a tartan motif around the rim.

'I'm not getting into the bed until you've taken it away,' you said. I told you not to be childish.

27

Holding your nose, you took it at arm's length to the back door and dropped it onto the flagstones in the yard, smashing it into curved chunks, like pelvic bones.

For two days we lay under an eiderdown on the sofa in front of a tiny wood stove, burning sticks of kindling, reading books, drinking whisky coffees and eating shortbread biscuits from a tin with Highland cattle on the lid. I slipped my hand down your sweat-pants and brought you to climax. Then you did the same for me. We didn't kiss or say anything. You turned away as I mopped myself and dropped the pieces of balled up pieces of toilet paper into the flames. Afterwards, we sat and watched the night filch down the loch, the rain scratching on the window and bleeding under the front door.

On the third day the forecast was better. We made a packed lunch and set off with a boy-scout map and compass hung around my neck. You'd never walked much further than to the shops in town. Your walking boots were new and squeaky. In the peaty swamps of the foothills I leapt from hillock to hillock. You stepped carefully around the black puddles of sucking mud.

'I feel like a mountain goat,' I said jumping further each time. Then I fell over and soaked my trousers. That was the first time you'd laughed in three days. You took a picture of me looking like a gamekeeper, all tweeds, gaiters and rucksack, staring onto the mountain tops.

We came to a rope-bridge over a fast-flowing river, swollen with recent rain. The bridge was only a foot above the muscular water as it raced to an inland loch. You wouldn't cross. To walk back the way we came would have added two hours to the hike. We were already tired. I tried cajoling you, reassuring you, shouting at you. You cried and said you couldn't do it. I walked back over the bridge onto the bank, grabbed your hand and pulled you into the water. You screamed at me. I pulled you through the water as it tugged up to our knees. I dragged you to the middle until you realised you weren't going to drown. Then you shook loose my hand and waded across the other half in front of me. You didn't stop on the far bank. There was a signpost back to the village. '5 miles' it said. You marched that five miles at a pace, a hundred yards ahead of me, head down, not a word spoken for almost two hours. The rain had started again.

We went to a local hotel for dinner that night. The Scottish hunting lodge experience here; waitresses in kilts, cobwebbed stag's heads, angry looking salmon in glass cases on the walls and wide, open fires, although the fires weren't lit.

After dinner we were led to a lounge where a fire had grudgingly been brought to life. I asked the wine waiter to leave a bottle of single malt on the side table. I, at last, found something semi-amusing to say about the rope-bridge. You, at last, half-smiled.

'I'm not walking another step tomorrow,' you said, 'and if you pull me into a river again, I'll fucking kill you.'

'What shall we do then?' I said. 'I'd planned another ten-miler.'

You shrugged your shoulders and picked a glossy magazine off a sideboard.

'How about we watch the rain coming under the door again,' you whispered.

I ploughed on through the whisky until they threw us out and you had to drive us back to the clap cold cottage.

We walked the beach again in the morning. You emptied your pocket of stones and shells onto the wet sand, except for one barnacled piece of quartz. You held it up to the sun's rays. The blue light shone into your eyes like a cold flame.

Fashion in Men's Footwear, Late 20th Century

The 1960s. With a shilling I can buy a stripy paper bag of lemon and lime chews. I watch the fat lady tip the sugary lipped jar over the pan on the scales. I scrutinise whilst she adds and subtracts sweets with her Liquorice Allsorts spade, until the big-hand points to four ounces-o-clock.

Outside, on her bicycle leant on the shop window, Pamela Blackwell has been holding my bike upright, her bare legs resting on her handlebars. I'd seen her red knickers as she pulled up her knees, so I squat down and re-tie the laces on my new black baseball boots.

On the path that leads to the woods I can't keep up with her. I breathe only the dust from her sherbet hair in the peppermint light that ripples through the leaves.

'If you give me all the red ones you can kiss me.' I think, for a shilling I could have bought a ton of strawberry hearts.

'There aren't any red ones,' I yell through tears, and wish that she'd notice my new black baseball boots.

I should be in the lead. I should be the one who decides what colour kisses are.

The 1970s. If I slide the driver's seat back as far as it can go, I can depress the clutch in my brown and cream, six-inch stacked platform shoes, although I can't feel if my right foot is on the miniscule brake or accelerator pedal.

Linda Osborne will be finishing her shift in the hotel restaurant at two-o-clock, just enough time for a pint in the bar. In her staff accommodation attic bedroom I unzip her out of her black waitress's skirt and unbutton her ironed white shirt. Her underwear smells of Sunday lunches.

'You're quite a bit shorter out of your shoes,' she says on her narrow bed.

Linda knows where there's a party. I double de-clutch the car through the lanes whilst I stroke the inside of her thigh. The right hand bend is thirty degrees too many. My stacked right foot presses on the accelerator rather than the brake. A ditch and a dry-stone wall come between us and the party.

'You fucking idiot, you nearly killed me,' she says before pulling down her denim skirt and climbing up the ditch to the road.

'Well I've broken a heel,' I tell her. 'And they cost thirty quid.'

The hotel chef arrives on his motorbike and helps Linda onto the pillion. I stand on my one good shoe so I'm as tall as he is.

The 1980s. In the gentlemen's outfitters in Oxford, where university students of philosophy purchase their English mustard corduroy trousers, I buy black Oxford shoes with loops of perforations around the shiny toe-caps. I've got a diploma in business studies from the polytechnic, but in London's square mile we're all high-flyers.

In the gentlemen's club in Soho we're measured up for girls and taxis hailed back to the company flat off Marble Arch. The fridge is stocked only with champagne. The boys take glasses and a bottle each, then peel off to the bedrooms where the girls peel off for their share of the bonuses.

But I can't go to the bedroom. I've fallen in love with Mandy who kisses me on the ear so softly, her hair as sheer and as black as her stockings. She tells me she's from Jamaica, and only does this work because her banker husband left her with two young kids, and there's the mortgage and the private school fees to pay, and the nanny when they're not boarding away. I start to make plans for when she and her children move in with me, and I help her

31

find a proper job, and we have two sweet, light brown kids of our own.

'Lover, are we going to do it or not?' she asks in the kitchen, after the champagne and the talk has dried up.

'No,' I say. 'I respect you too much for that.' and 'Can we meet outside of work any time soon, somewhere non-business related, as it were?'

'After work next Monday,' she says. 'But I need something to make up for lost income tonight.'

I give her a hundred and open the cab door for her in the sober London dawn.

'You're a proper gentleman,' she says and kisses me.

I look down at my black Oxfords. Yes, I think, I am.

'We haven't got any Jamaican Mandys here. Never had,' says the doorman of the gentlemen's club on the Monday night.

I tip the shoeshine boy a fiver and buy new laces I don't need.

The 1990s. The sun boils into the beach buggy my fiancée Alison and I have hired for the day. I drive in bare feet even though the foot pedals are too hot to touch.

We drive through villages where children's faces watch our passing from glassless windows and baking stoops. Down a track that leads through breadfruit and banyan trees, the children run after us, shoeless over the sharp road-stone. White sand arcs round the green water and black shadows of coral. We leave the buggy in the shade of eucalyptus and take beach bags.

We lay our hotel towels under coconut trees and walk the length of the beach, hand in hand. I stop and throw fallen coconuts into the waves. We watch them bobbing like swimmers' heads and wait for them to roll back up the sand. We've brought a picnic of wine and pink melons. I cut the melons with a knife borrowed from the hotel's buffet. I try to stab drinking holes in a coconut but miss and stab a hole in her towel.

'I hope I don't get stranded on a desert island with you,' Alison says.

'We should go for a swim now we're here,' I say. 'Skinny dipping. We're the only ones on the beach.'

'No way,' she says, and asks me to hold her towel whilst she pulls on a one-piece.

'Reminds me of family holidays in Newquay,' I say.

She won't go into the sea. 'It's too coral-ly and I didn't bring shoes.'

Alison goes back into the shade and rubs in more high-factor. I do breaststroke over the warm swell. Two local girls come onto the beach and strip off at the water's edge. Under dirty dresses they're wearing bikinis but they toss the tops aside then high step over the waves. In the deeper water they arch their bodies then disappear under, their bottoms floating momentarily on the surface. I go back to the towels and stretch out. She's pretending to be asleep behind sunglasses. I close my eyes and listen to the two girls chattering like the frantic little birds in the papaya trees.

Then there's a heavy wet slap on my stomach. I don't look up.

'Ouch, what the hell was that for?'

'What was what for?'

I look up. There's a lizard on me, rat-sized, but with a longer tail. It's fallen, or jumped, from the coconut tree leaning over us. It turns its head to one side and winks at me.

'Fucking Hell!' I jump to my feet, flaying at my stomach. The back of my hand touches the lizard's mouth.

'Arrgh, I felt its flicky tongue.'

Alison starts to laugh. I haven't seen her laugh since we arrived. I'm not sure I have ever seen Alison laugh like she is now.

'Serves you right. Those girls felt your 'flicky tongue' when you swam up close.'

The lizard slinks into the undergrowth. I watch the girls skip out of the water and dress. They don't have towels but the water evaporates from their brown skin. When they walk past us, they're dry as pebbles.

'We should make love now we're here,' I say to Alison. 'Deserted tropical beach, coconut trees…'

'And have a reptile crawl over me? No thanks.'

We don't speak on the walk back to the buggy. Alison strides in front of me with her towel wrapped from her chest down. The top of the dashboard, behind the steering wheel, has been adorned with red and pink seashells and blooms of wild hibiscus.

'Gifts from the children,' I say, and pull my camera from the beach bag. 'Put a flower behind your ear. Take the towel off. Let me take a photo.'

She picks a compact mirror from her bag and smears sun block on her nose. 'Save it for the local fauna,' she says.

One by one, my fiancée drops the seashells and hibiscus flowers into our slipstream. I stop at a roadside shack that has beach things for sale on a wooden trestle.

'I'm going to buy a pair of jelly shoes,' I say. 'I'm getting cold feet.'

She raises her sunglasses. 'Jelly shoes? Jelly shoes,' she says, 'are for wankers.'

Nap of the Cloth

Fifty-five years is a stretch to know someone as a friend. Okay, there are some who glue themselves together that long in marriage, but as a friend. Fifty-five years is a long time as a friend.

'Fifty-five years,' we say, and shake our heads, glasses to our lips.

We take turns to pick the hotel. He goes for the exclusive country house. I've kept up, hidden the bills from my wife. He scrunches his classic Jaguar up the gravel driveway. I've parked my hatchback around the back by the kitchen bins.

I compliment him on his shoes, gleaming black with a splinter buckle. He tells me the shoemaker's Italian name which I pretend to know. He tells me he bought them off an internet auction for half the normal price.

'I wear dead men's designer shoes. You should try it,' he says and hands me the menu. 'You order.'

He reckons I know more about food than he does. I think we're both relieved there's something. He says he's never heard of bouillabaisse.

'Fish stew,' I say. 'Let's try it. We can't eat fish at home. My wife's lips swell up.'

He selects champagne from the list. I could buy wine-in-a-box to last me three weeks with the same money.

Over our bouillabaisse we talk about our respective offspring. His are straight A students, all still at home. He pays £300 a week to keep two refrigerators topped up with organic food. Mine have decent enough jobs in hospitality.

'We get on with them fine now they've gone,' I say.

We talk about our wives over the main courses. Parts of their bodies they've lost over the years and some they've gained. How long since we were intimate with them.

'Things are pretty good in that department,' he says.

'We don't sleep in the same bedroom,' I say.

He tells me about his affair with a work colleague. I tell him about the affair I nearly had. We tell the waitress how much we enjoyed the fish.

The conversation turns to sex, which lasts through dessert and cheeseboard. We go over old ground. When we shared a flat, we did alright. We replay names and faces. Girls that stayed for a night or a year. His girlfriends were beautiful. Mine – more on the quirky side.

'It's all going to change,' he says. 'Doctor gave me some bad news last week.' He looks in the direction of his lap.

'Mate, I'm sorry. Curable nowadays?'

'Depends on your luck,' he says.

We ask for coffee to be taken in the snooker room. We toss a coin, chalk the cues, run our palms over the nap.

This is how it was. Friday night, clean shirts, pressed jeans, best of three frames before the pubs open. Reggae music in the snooker club, smoke-filled, low hanging lights. Adrenalin high, expectation higher. In the morning, kitchen table post-mortems of the night before over bacon and egg sandwiches. We were equals then with everything to play for.

Fragaria Vesca

Soon after they set off on the hill walk, Alan spotted some wild strawberries – dimpled drops of blood-red spattered under the hedge. They stopped and picked all they could find, which wasn't many – perhaps a dozen each.

'I honestly didn't know such things existed,' Constance said.

'*Fragaria Vesca,* sometimes known as *Sow's Teats*,' he said.

Alan was a keen amateur forager. He'd started seriously hunting for wild food after his wife left, when there was just him, a stout stick and a weekend country walk. His ex had never appreciated the brambleberries or sloes he'd harvested from their garden hedges. 'Bird food' she'd called it.

'*Fragaria Vesca* has the more romantic ring,' Constance said. 'Not that I'll be foraging for romance anytime soon.'

Alan had put together a folder on his computer with recipes for wild food, all foraged from local hedgerows, ponds and woods. Wild garlic, wild mushrooms, wild asparagus. His recipe for cream of stinging-nettle soup had been printed in the local paper when they'd run a feature on garden recycling.

'Let's save the sow's teats to eat with our dessert,' Alan said. 'They'll be something to look forward to.'

They'd booked a table for a pub lunch after the hill walk. She found room for the delicate finds next to her homemade fruitcake in the plastic container she'd brought.

Constance had read that from the summit of their hill-walk, there were wonderful, far-reaching views and, on a day like today, they'd be able to see across the floodplains of the silver river, to the bridge, and mountains beyond.

'Apparently it's not obvious when you've reached the top,' she said. 'There's nothing to say you've arrived.' They stopped to gather breath. Since leaving Alan's car in the lane outside the pub, the incline had been relentlessly uphill.

'Can you hear the grasshoppers?' he asked.

'I read something about an iron-age hillfort. If we find one, we're on the right track.'

'The male grasshopper chirps as loudly as he can, and the females respond with a similar sounding song. They're considered a delicacy in Uganda.' Alan looked at the OS map hung around his neck in a transparent map-carrier. 'There's a way to go yet before we reach any fortifications.'

They'd met through an internet dating site. It had been Alan's last throw of the dice before his half-price three-monthly membership expired. Constance had been the only one who'd answered his volley of introductory chirps.

They sat on the grass with their backs to a dry-stone wall. The dark spinney on the other side of the wall offered them protection from the midday sun. Constance delved into her little rucksack and pulled out a bottle of lukewarm, Icelandic glacier water.

'A perfect spot for fruitcake,' she said. Alan had known she'd be upper-class when he'd spotted her on the dating-site. Something about her Alice band and sensible flat shoes. Her profile picture showed her standing in a doorway that could have been a stately home.

'My great grandfather sold his castle in Scotland to the Queen Mother,' she'd told Alan. Alan's great grandfather had been a coal-miner in the Rhondda. He'd shown Constance a photograph of his forebears' gravestones he'd found outside a boarded-up Methodist chapel near Barry Island. That was during his genealogy period which pre-dated the onset of foraging.

'I'm not sure we have enough in common, Alan,'

Constance had emailed him after that first date in the vegan café. 'I enjoy a lamb chop once in a while.'

'We're both looking for companionship, aren't we?' he'd replied, and she'd agreed to meet him for a second date on a country walk.

'Nothing ventured...' she'd said.

Constance had suggested the hill walk and pub venues. Alan volunteered to do the driving and bought an Ordnance Survey map. He'd revised the exact route they'd take on several occasions. He'd felt that getting lost or being late for their lunchtime booking would go against him.

Constance snapped the lid back on the empty cake container and they continued up the hill. She told him about her late husband's illness. How he'd not known who she was, holding her hand on his deathbed. Alan reached out a comforting hand as he could see a tear in her eye. She looked at Alan's hand but didn't take it.

'Enough about me,' she said. 'What's happening in your life?'

'I've put in for voluntary redundancy,' Alan said. 'I'm going into full-time foraging. I've applied for a stall on a farmer's market.'

'Is there much call for wild food? Will you make enough money to live on?'

'People are turning back to Mother Nature. A jar of crab-apple jelly is something they can believe in. Besides, I'm not doing it for the money; I'm finally going to do something I enjoy.'

'I believe in my monthly supermarket vouchers. Besides, I enjoy doing my online shop,' Constance said. 'My late husband used to say, "Money might not make you happy, but it gives you options." He was able to afford the Rolls-Royce of coffins.'

'I think this is the hillfort you were talking about,' Alan

said. 'You can make out the ditches and ramparts to repel invaders.'

'So this is the top?'

'Downhill all the way from here. Unless you want to go "off-piste" for a stretch?'

'We're too old to stray from the footpath.'

'As a full-time forager, I'll be forging many a new path through the undergrowth.'

Constance unrolled her pac-a-mac and lay down on it. Alan sat up, looking at the view over the distant river as it looped towards the sea.

'It's probably not often you can see the bridge,' he said, but Constance didn't answer, she'd closed her eyes.

'We'll have to imagine it,' she said.

Alan looked down at her shapely figure and imagined a shared future. He thought about lying down next to her and explaining the joys of naked foraging. Instead, he rose and wondered around the mounds and valleys of the hillfort. He picked cornflowers and columbine, cow parsley and kingcup and made a little posy tied with a long length of grass. He took them back to Constance who was scrolling through messages on her phone.

'As a thank you for coming today.'

'You are sweet. Am I meant to eat them?'

'I could find you an edible bunch. Wild salads are an excellent source of free radicals.'

'I'll make do with a bit of iceberg and cress at the pub.'

On the way back down the hill they pointed things out to each other. A buzzard patrolling the unbroken blue sky, a replanted orchard with young apple trees, a field of fattening lambs slowing in the shade. They heard a stream as it chased them, overgrown with bramble, and they paused to savour the fragrance of some pink dog-roses. Alan stopped and rubbed the leaves of a tall weed between his fingers.

'*Jack-in-the-Hedge*. A mustardy, garlic flavour,' he said. 'A wild alternative to spinach.'

'After how many dogs have cocked a leg on it, I wonder?'

Catching her unawares, Alan swooped his hand into hers. She let his fingers intertwine and for a minute accepted her fate like a field mouse in the shadow of a buzzard's wing. As the pub came into view, her hand wriggled for freedom and Alan released.

They were the only ones in the pub-garden and shared the same wooden bench on one side of the table.

'Shall we have some shade?' Alan stood and pulled the cord on the large red sun umbrella.

'I was looking forward to some warmth on my face,' Constance said and moved to the other side of the table. 'But you stay there if you'd rather.'

A waitress brought them menus and took their orders for drinks. They studied the lunchtime choices in silence. They both agreed that it all looked tempting, and they'd enjoy any of it if it weren't for the prohibitive prices.

'Choose anything you fancy,' Alan said. 'This one's on me.'

'I'd rather pay my own way. Isn't that what the dating site advises? Share the costs until you get to know each other?'

'I feel as though I do know you.'

'After a morning coffee and a hill walk?'

'Well, leave room for the wild strawberries. They're free if nothing else.'

The waitress came to take their food orders. They decided to pass on the starters, and both plumped for something mid-to-low range from the mains.

The Lake

There were five of us on the path to the lake; Jordi and me on bikes, Marigold and the twins, Lakyn and Cassia, on foot. The girls candied up in skimpy summer shorts with their scarlet lipstick, night club hair and bra straps thumbed out from under sleeveless t-shirts.

The path was wide enough for the girls to walk side by side, with us boys showing off, pulling wheelies and skidding our rear wheels in the blanket of wild garlic, crushing up a pungency to compete with the girl's cheap perfume. The girls feigned indifference, little handbags slung over their bare shoulders, arms crossed over budding breasts. They'd stopped halfway and sat in a line on a dry stone wall. Jordi and I lent our bikes against the stones and perched one on each end.

The bright eye of the sun shone through the wood's spring canopy, onto a ringing mass of bluebells and herds of cow parsley. Birdsong flooded the woods with more than sound, it was like you could reach out to the valley waking from hibernation and stroke the top of its head. For a moment we were silent. Our eyes followed the line of the stream as it threaded down to where we were born, each one of us hoping to see a future as far away from the village as possible. I'd stretched my fingers along the wall as close as I dare to Marigold's bare thigh. My heart stopped when her fingers touched mine.

A tree had keeled over from the lake's bank, its smooth, leafless branches rising from the water like serpents. Jordi knelt at the water's edge, cupped both hands and scooped out tadpoles. He let the water sieve from his fingers until the black sperm wriggled their fragile tails in his palms.

'We have to go for a swim,' Cassia said.

'In our clothes?' I said.

Lakyn and Cassia had already dropped their handbags and taken off their shoes.

'Just take your tops off,' Lakyn said. 'We'll be dry by the time we've walked back.'

Three of us watched as the twins pulled off their t-shirts. I'd never seen a bra over real breasts. Cassia's was yellow, Lakyn's was pink – delicate as cut flowers. I was sure I could smell roses.

'I'm going back,' said Marigold.

'Don't go Mari,' the twins yelled.

'You're both sluts.' She was crying.

'She's wearing a see-through bra, that's why,' Lakyn said.

'She's got nothing to put in a bra,' Cassia said.

I went after her. 'You don't have to go swimming Marigold,' I said. 'Please stay.'

'If you go swimming with them, we're finished,' she said and walked on.

I let her go, stunned to hear that we'd started.

Jordi and I took off our t-shirts and jeans. The freezing water weighed around us like armour. Our feet sank into the silt on the bottom then, in the space of one stride, we were out of our depth. The four of us swam to the fallen tree and hung onto the branches. Shrieking with cold, we skimmed sheets of water over each other until, in unison, the twins arched their bodies and went under, their bottoms floating momentarily on the surface.

Jordi and I were first out of the water and took the twins' hands, pulling them up the bank, doing our best not to look down their wet underwear. We pulled on clothes, Jordi and I in silence, the twins chattering as though nothing had just happened.

On the way back through the woods we stopped at the derelict cottage. There were mildewed signs screwed into the stonework that said 'Danger – Unsafe Structures'. The doors had thick fencing posts nailed horizontally across the frames. The glass in the rusted mullioned window frames had been smashed years before. We peered through at abandoned lives. There was a wooden-handled grindstone wheel and the remains of a horse-drawn log carriage. In the corner were steep, wooden stairs to the first floor.

'I've always wanted to go up those stairs.' Lakyn said.

'There's no way in.' I replied.

Cassia moved round to one of the wooden doors and pointed to where it should have reached the ground. There was a gap between the bottom of the rotted panels and the earth. Jordi pulled at the crumbling wood. Pieces came away in his hands – enough to crawl under.

Downstairs, there was nothing more to see. I turned the handle on the grindstone till it hummed, then burnt my hand trying to stop it. With her feet feeling the sturdiness of the wood, Lakyn climbed the stairs. I went into one bedroom with her, Jordi into another with Cassia. The bare floorboards were pasted with bird shit and putrefying, feathered ribcages. There was a disturbed flapping from exposed roof timbers as roosting pigeons clattered their escape. Lakyn put her lips up to mine. I tasted lake mud on her tongue. She put her hand behind my head and pulled me tight onto her face. I put my hand between her legs and felt under her wet shorts.

We walked out of the beech woods in the late afternoon sunlight, Jordi and I attempting to push along our bikes with our arms around the twins. I looked anywhere but at Lakyn. The great brushes of ivy that choked the trees darkened and solidified as the sun fell down the sky. Ladders of fungi swirled up the fence posts and along the fallen timber. I stopped once or twice to pull stones out of the high mud banks, looking for ammonite fossils as I'd done as a kid.

When we were in sight of the twins' house they let go of our hands and ran on ahead. By the time Jordi and I reached their front door it was shut.

Lakyn and Cassia went on to the same university then shared a flat in London. I saw them in the village pub years later. They'd been to visit their parents. They shouted my name and kissed me. Made me feel I was someone for a while.

Marigold was married with a baby daughter by the time she was twenty-three, divorced and a single mum by the time she was twenty-eight. I invited her out for drink once, but we couldn't think of a damn thing to say once we'd reminisced over our school days together.

When it came to saying goodbye she wept and said, 'Whatever happened to us?'

And me? I never got away. I still live in the same village. I do some labouring on building sites, some landscape gardening. Hand to mouth. I'm allowed to see my son once a fortnight.

At the weekend I walk the dog to the lake. When it's hot she goes in the water after a stick. The derelict cottage is still standing, although the rotten stairs were removed on grounds of safety. The pigeons have the bedrooms to themselves now; finding a mate, nurturing their chicks, piling up the shit and the dead.

The Dead Dog Tree

We halt our walk for you to look at The Dead Dog Tree. Hanging by sodden, redundant dog-leads, rain-filled wallets of clear plastic with smudged photos of deceased canines. We were going to scatter our dog's ashes here but never got around to it. I poured them onto the compost heap. I lied and said I'd poured them under the copper beech tree, but you've never let me forget it anyway. You read each card and your eyes well up. Some of them you've almost memorized.

The steep embankments of the Iron Age fort encircle two or three golf greens. Patchwork shapes of mown green velvet spotted amongst the wholemeal brown of the thick, long grass. Numbered flags thwacking in the gusts. You're wearing woolly hats now. The wig made your head hot and itchy. Made you cry when you looked in the mirror. I didn't tell you it was a faint shade of mauve, not 'gorgeous grey'. We walk down through the gauges from when stone was quarried here. You loved our thick stone walled house until I told you I didn't. Until I said it was a prison.

We cross the fairway, a swathe of tiny blue flowers.

'Forget-me-nots,' I say, then try and recapture the words. You take a picture of a tree with your phone.

'I want to plant one in the garden,' you say. 'Somewhere you could hang pictures.'

A wooden finger sign by the fallen down dry stone wall. 'Bridleway, club house, footpath.' We found a filigree earring in the fallen stone wall in the garden. We were going to take the ear-ring to the museum but lost it. You said it wasn't lost.

'It's returned to the spirit world,' you said.

Spirits have become a fixture since your diagnosis. You've hung wind chimes outside the windows so we can hear them come and go.

We climb towards the trig point at the highest part of the fort, walk over the cinder footpaths with arrows pointing to tee and flag numbers. What number chemo session are we on? I should know this, so don't ask. From here we can see the bright ribbon of river as it bends towards the sea.

'High tide for a change,' I say. 'We only ever seem to be here at low.'

You're sitting on the old metal bench, half buried in undergrowth. You stop here for breath before the short, muddy climb to the top. You aim your phone camera at a pair of kestrels floating on the wind.

'Things will change after this,' you say.

We trace our fingers over the arrows in the metal map on the top of the trig point. You run your fingernail along the groove pointing to our village, our house. For me, things have already changed.

You close your eyes. Spread your arms out wide like wings.

Puffballs

I first saw her from the bedroom window. She was wearing wellington boots and a shiny new waxed jacket. Her bright red and pink harem pants weren't the usual attire for hikers. Her burnt orange hair was piled into a loose and low chignon that spilt onto her shoulders. I could see she was attractive, but sensed she didn't pay it any attention, like a brightly coloured butterfly settled on an ordinary leaf.

An arthritic Labrador dog lagged behind her. I watched her stroll across the wet-grassed meadow, stop for the dog to relieve himself and then wait while he sniffed at the left-behind scents of fox and badger. I thought she was probably staying in one of the village holiday-lets, a city-dweller up from London for a long weekend.

She fell into a regular pattern of morning and afternoon walks, following the footpath that ran the length of my cottage garden. My work desk was set below the bedroom window, so I rarely missed her excursions. I noticed her picking wild field mushrooms into a small netted bag. In the right conditions they thrived in the lengthening September shadows. On the fourth afternoon she looked up at me and smiled. Embarrassed to have been noticed, I smiled back and lifted a hand.

Although exercising the dog had fallen into a routine for her, it became something of a disturbance for me. My concentration on the computer became diverted by any dog-walker that might have been her.

On the fifth day I resolved to be outside, to set the stage for a 'chance' meeting. At nine-o-clock I began to collect fallen twigs from underneath the beech that stretched over the footpath. I'd tell her that I was hoarding kindling for the wood-burner.

By quarter past she still hadn't walked up the footpath.

By half past I'd picked the lawn clean of everything. Back at my work desk I was restless and distracted. I made endless cups of tea. From the kitchen window I could see the footpath where it crossed in front of the garden gate.

That afternoon I went outside again. This time I found secateurs and began chopping at the roses. I'd nearly given up when she came into view, crossing the meadow. She must have walked her circular route in the opposite direction. I chose my moment to break off from the dead-heading and ambled into the footpath. I squatted and stroked her dog.

'Hello, you're a lovely old lad aren't you,' I said, ruffling the dog's ears. 'What's his name?'

'Toffee,' she said. 'He hasn't been well. His poor old legs.'

I thought she was mid-forties, making me ten years older. Her only makeup was some pale pink lip-gloss. Her hair was swirled into the same loose bun that seemed both coiffured and quickly constructed – as though in the morning after something formal. Her voice was soft with a faint Mediterranean accent, Italian or Spanish.

'You're a new face,' I said. 'Here on holiday? I'm Peter by the way.'

'No, we've moved here short term. We're renting Parsley Cottage. I'm Bea.'

Parsley Cottage was half a mile away. Years ago, it had been the village shop and post office.

'We, as in you and Toffee?'

'And Greg my husband, but he spends most of his time in London or abroad. I'm meant to be house-hunting.'

'Sorry, I'm being nosey.'

'No. You're the first local who's spoken to me. What about you. Been here long?'

'Ten years. Live alone. My grown-up daughter drops in occasionally. How are you finding it?'

'Peaceful. Good for mushrooms.'

'I suppose that's why I came,' I said. 'The quiet.'

It was at that point that Toffee collapsed to the ground, as though settling down to sleep on the muddy footpath.

'Oh no, I'll never be able to get him up again,' she said, 'I've walked him too far.' She tried coaxing him back to his feet, but he wasn't going anywhere.

'Shall I get my car? We can lift him into the back, and I'll drive you home,' I said.

'Would you mind? I'm sorry to trouble to you like this.'

I managed to lift the old dog from my car into Parsley Cottage as Bea held the door. She pointed to his basket in the kitchen.

'He'll get up eventually,' she said. 'Greg says he'll make the hard decision when Toffee doesn't get up.'

While she made coffee, I told Bea what I did; a self-employed accountant. Small businesses mainly. Something I could do from home. I came to the village after my wife left.

She told me Greg was a foreign correspondent for a national newspaper, that she was his second wife, and that she met him in Dubrovnik during the Yugoslav wars. He was the intrepid reporter. She was the young translator.

'We're a living, breathing cliché,' she said.

They owned a flat in central London, but her husband dreamt of reliving his childhood in the English countryside.

'I'm lonely in London and even lonelier here,' Bea said.

'There's not a lot happening. Will you find work?'

'Greg's against it. He says Toffee will keep me company while he's away.'

I let a few days go by without talking again to Bea. I made sure I was at my desk at the times she took Toffee for his walks. Much shorter now. Up the footpath, across the meadow and back. I willed the dog to collapse again, but he limped on. We waved at each other sometimes. I began to wonder what I was doing in that grim cottage. It hadn't been decorated since the 80s and was cold and damp in the winter. Mine was a solitary, silent, non-existence. I'd been to Dubrovnik, to Croatia. Who'd want to live in some dreary English backwater?

At the end of the second, restless week, I pulled on my boots and waited for her on the footpath.

'Mind if I join you for some fresh air?'

'Please do. You'll be the first person I've spoken to in days.'

'Not even your husband?'

'Strictly text only when Greg's at work. Those are my orders.'

After that, I walked with Bea and Toffee two or three times a week. I wished then that Toffee had been a young pup, able to walk for miles. I often thought about asking Bea out for lunch, or in for supper, but I was afraid of spoiling something.

The last day I saw her properly, she was walking down the path with what looked like a white football under her arm. I went out to meet her.

'A giant puffball,' she said. 'I've heard about them, but never found or eaten one'

'I'm told they're delicious. Had breakfast?'

She came into my home for the first time and sat at the kitchen table while I sliced up the puffball and fried it. Neither of us had eaten with another human being for weeks. We sat and recounted our life stories till lunchtime, when Bea said she had to go.

'Greg's booked a call to discuss progress on the house-hunting,' she told me. 'I haven't even been trying.'

'I hope you'll stay in the area,' I said. 'What would I do without Toffee?'

When she left, she held both my hands and kissed me. I felt short of breath for the remainder of the day and couldn't work. I sat for hours at the kitchen table, dreaming up impossible plans.

She knocked on the door early the next morning.

'He wants me back in London,' she said. 'I'll be catching the afternoon train.'

'When will you be back?' I asked.

'When he says, I suppose.'

I took to following her steps up the footpath and across the meadow as though retracing her route would somehow bring her back.

Puffballs don't last that long. They dehydrate, discolour and shrivel. If you hit them with a stick, they explode into clouds of green smoke. I think that's the spores, drifting off to germinate somewhere else.

Giants

For you, the best part of our honeymoon were the giant tortoises. You'd collect lettuce leaves off the hotel's buffet table in your handbag, then go to the tropical gardens that surrounded our bedroom veranda. You'd feed the tortoise's Neanderthal faces and stroke the warm mahogany houses on their backs, as if they could feel your caresses. You convinced me their shells were finely attuned to touch.

For me, the best part of our honeymoon was winning on the roulette table the night we arrived. I put a hundred pounds on number 10 – the date we got married. We won enough to pay for the trip. Then, over the next three nights, you sat beside me at the tables, head on my shoulder, turning to the light the jewel I'd put on your finger. And I turned you to the light, for other men to wonder at. I lost every penny.

We'd drink pink wine at lunchtime, in the heat of the sun, then return to our room. We didn't have much to pull off each other – a bikini, a pair of swim shorts. You'd fondle between my legs and say it reminded you of a tortoise's neck and head. All it needed was a grasping mouth. I'd walk into the bedroom from the shower and see the outline of your nakedness on the huge white bed, the mosquito nets blurring your breasts and limbs, your face turned to the open window. The giant tortoises were calling. Their sad, low-pitched mating groans that shook the foundations.

Paunch Porsche Pooch

Susannah listened to her younger work colleagues in the office talk about love in the same way she listened to people talk about the paranormal. She experienced the same lurid fascination, the same scepticism, and the same wish that if only it would happen to her, then she'd believe.

'The clock is ticking,' her sister chimed, when they met for lunch on Susannah's recent birthday.

'Don't be ridiculous,' Susannah said. 'The clock stopped ticking years ago and, as far as I know, they haven't found a way of rewinding women of our "certain age", have they?'

'I didn't mean that particular clock, Dear,' her sister said, emptying the half bottle of wine into their glasses. 'You still have time to fall in love. Just about.'

Susannah wondered what on earth her sister knew about love. Her sister hadn't married out of love, she'd married because she'd been desperate to leave their parents' suffocating home, have sex with her then fiancée, and buy a three-piece suite. Her sister had confided that the three-piece suite had far outlasted the sex. Susannah had made an early decision to wait for the real 'love' thing. It had already been a long wait.

'You're internet savvy.' Her sister caught the waiter's eye and scribbled into the air for the bill. 'Have you tried any of the dating sites? My hairdresser met her partner online and tied the knot within a year. They drove to Bognor Regis one bank holiday weekend and asked the owner of the B&B to be their witness at the registry office.'

'I'd rather take Holy Orders and become a nun.'

Susannah was lying. She'd tried several dating sites and even added the monthly charges onto her household budget spreadsheet. She'd been dismayed by how many ageing men insisted on posing bare-chested in front of their open-top cars, often holding onto some poor dog, as if to say, "Look at me, I possess all we need to fall in love." She called it the 'Paunch Porsche Pooch' factor. The last man she'd met via a dating site was so old she'd had to help him up the steps into the pub. He'd admitted to routinely lying about his age and posting old photos onto his profile to attract a younger woman.

'What I lack in youth, I make up for in other departments.' He'd simultaneously squeezed his wallet and crotch.

Susannah had excused herself after gulping down one drink, and when she returned home, blocked him on the dating site. She'd already blocked most of the other men in a fifty mile radius, after reading their excruciating intros.

'Look after yourself, Dear,' her sister said. They hugged and air-kissed each other on the cheek in the car park. 'I worry about you, sitting on your own every night. Join a walking group. You never know who you might meet while keeping fit. You're looking a bit peaky.'

She'd tried walking groups too. The truth was, she didn't have the energy anymore. The distances were more than she could comfortably manage without losing her puff, or wanting to pee, or both. That was why her next stop after the restaurant, was her doctor's surgery.

'There's more to life than men,' she said, searching her handbag for her car keys.

Susannah wished she hadn't chosen the waiting-room chair directly facing the clock. It was a modern looking, utilitarian clock. Square, with a black plastic rim, large black numbers, and three unadorned black clock hands. She calculated that the second hand took eighteen seconds to pass over the name of the medicine advertised on the lower half of the clock face. She looked up the medicine on her mobile phone. Irritable bowels. Perhaps that was her trouble. Irritable everything. She'd now been waiting for thirty-eight minutes past her appointment time. She'd give it forty-five minutes then say she had another pressing appointment to go to. She didn't, but it was worth making the point. Her previous doctor had never kept her waiting, but Janet (they'd been on first name terms) had recently retired, lucky woman. The name of her new doctor, whom she hadn't yet met, was Harpreet Singh, a man. She'd felt embarrassed asking the receptionist which gender, but she hadn't encountered the name 'Harpreet' before.

'Susannah Morris, please.' The doctor poked his head into the waiting room on the forty-third minute. She rose from her chair and moved towards the door. She could see him watching her straighten up from the slight stoop she'd recently developed when sitting for too long. 'Hello, I'm Doctor Singh. Apologies for the wait.' They shook hands.

'No problem at all.' She followed his tall figure down the short corridor to a pale wooden door with his name in the clear plastic slot. The light blue of his turban matched the blue of his tie, which for some reason had flipped over his left shoulder. She thought that perhaps he'd just been washing his hands, which would account for his right hand's warmth in her permanently icy palm.

The doctor waited for her to take a seat at the side of his desk, before seating himself and swivelling his chair to face her.

'Pleased to meet you, Miss Morris. I've taken over Dr Janet Evan's patient list.'

'Please call me Susannah. Janet always did.'

'Susannah it is. And I'm Harpreet.'

She dragged her eyes away from Harpreet's smile. His

flawless teeth were as white as his pressed shirt, and although his greying beard indicated he was around the same age as her, there was a smoothness to his skin that should have belonged to a younger man. She tried to concentrate on the vitamin chart pinned on the noticeboard behind the doctor's chair.

'What can I do for you today?'

Susannah told him about her aches and pains, her tiredness and tetchiness, her little lumps and bumps. 'I think I might be depressed,' she said. 'Who isn't, these days?'

Sitting on his couch, undressed to her briefs, she watched the second hand on the clock above the desk as his hand moved slowly over each of her breasts. She'd declined his offer of a female nurse chaperone. She hadn't reached her age without knowing how to look after herself, she thought.

'Have you been through the menopause?' he asked.

'The change of life didn't seem to change mine,' she answered. She breathed in surreptitious lungfuls of his aroma and studied the fine silk weave of his turban. The brand of medicine on his clock wasn't the same as on the waiting-room clock. He asked her to lie on the couch while he felt her lower abdomen, inside her armpits, and around her throat and neck. Did Sikhs wear wedding rings? His fingers were bare.

'Please get dressed, then we'll take some bloods before you go.'

While she dressed, she wondered why she'd never been to India. She'd always wanted to. The Indian people were all so – well, 'lovable'. Gentle, polite, intelligent, good looking.

'I'm going to request a hospital appointment for you,' he said. 'I think we need a full body scan, just so we know what to discount.'

57

'What part of India are you from?' Susannah asked. She'd known all along that hospital would be on the cards. 'I've always wanted to visit.'

'I was born in North London, but my parents came from Amritsar in the Punjab.'

'I'm sorry… I didn't mean to assume… to be impolite.' Tears were running down her face.

'Don't worry about anything, Susannah.' He handed her a tissue from a box on his desk.

She saw Harpreet at the surgery quite regularly after the diagnosis. He told her he was a widower, living alone. Grown up children. All of them medics. She wished she could've plucked up the courage to ask him back to hers for a cup of tea, or around for supper. She would when all this was over. Perhaps they could accompany each other to the Punjab.

When the nurse had said, "There's a handsome Indian gentleman in reception, come to visit you," she'd known right away who it was. She and Harpreet chatted for ages, but now she was tired. He held her hand while they enjoyed a few moments silence. She watched the minute hand of the clock on the wall of her single-occupancy room moving towards half past, the time he said he'd have to be on his way. There was no sponsor's name on this clock. Susannah raised her hand off the blanket and pointed.

'Look, no miracle cure to buy a little more time.'

But Harpreet had slipped away a little earlier than planned.

The Leopard Cup

Through the mullioned window behind his small desk, Trevor watched the young couple enter the castle grounds. Holding hands, the pair were wrapped up in winter coats and scarves, although for an early January day the mid-afternoon sun was unnaturally warm. A daytime crescent moon floated low and bright over the mountain. Trevor wished he had his camera. A photograph of the moon above the mountain, above the crumbling battlements of the castle may have been worthy of a competition entry. Since the tremors started, Trevor didn't take as many photographs. Neither his hands or head were still enough. Setting up the tripod was all too much of a palaver and lacked the spontaneity for the best shots.

Trevor worked at the Castle Museum every Sunday, Wednesday and Friday. He was one of three key holders whose duty it was to open the doors at 10am, lock up at 4pm and staff the desk in the interim. There were no admission fees to worry about and the modest cash float for the postcards and trinkets was kept in a shoebox safe in the curator's basement office. Well, more of a cubby-hole than an office.

Trevor looked at his watch. If the couple wanted to look around the museum, they'd better be quick; he'd be shutting up shop in an hour. He hoped they would venture in; it had been a quiet day. Sharing his knowledge of the displays made it worthwhile.

The museum housed over fifty thousand artefacts but only displayed one tenth of that number. Trevor knew every single item by name. He'd spent two years cataloguing them from handwritten ledgers onto his home computer. He'd found three of the relics himself. That was over ten years ago. He'd been walking his dog along the canal path and, just for the hell of it, he'd knocked his walking-stick against a trunk of a willow tree. He'd stopped walking when the noise sounded strangely hollow. He'd knocked again. The sound was like that of a small drum, the tree bark stretched over a resonant cavity. He'd speared the hollow area with the sharp end of his stick and its shaft had disappeared six inches into the trunk. When Trevor had prized and peeled away the bark, he'd found three bronze axe-heads. He'd taken them straight to the museum. That had been his first visit, even though he'd lived in the town all his life.

The couple walked through the narrow doorway and said hello. English accents. Trevor didn't like the English. English visitors to the museum had a way of being condescending and faintly amused when they discovered that Wales had a history distinct from its overbearing neighbour. Trevor had ventured into England only once in all his seventy years: to London, on the train, to visit the British Museum. All five of the town museum's staff had gone together on a 'fact-finding' mission. He couldn't recall what facts they'd found – if any. One of the five had been his wife, Angharad. She'd looked after the museum's collection of vintage clothing, painstakingly restoring the threadbare knitwear and lace. Neither of them knew she had less than a year.

Trevor had wanted all the exhibit labels in the Castle Museum to be printed in the Welsh language above the English, but he'd been over-ruled by the bossy woman from Welsh Heritage in Cardiff.

'English is the first language of the Welsh and the second language of most foreign tourists to the town,' she'd lectured him. Trevor couldn't speak Welsh himself, but he could pronounce Welsh place names in a near perfect accent.

The couple went first to the display case of pots, urns and Roman coins. In pride of place was the Roman bronze 'Leopard Cup'. The cup had been found just a few miles from the town. A subsequent archaeological dig had determined the site had once been an important cremation and burial plot. The cup's handle was an exquisitely carved leopard inlaid with silver, with amber beads as the eyes. In fact, the Leopard Cup had been substituted in the display case with a large colour photograph of the real thing. The actual article itself had, in Trevor's view, been purloined by Cardiff Museum. The same bossy woman from Welsh Heritage had said that the security in the town's Castle Museum was insufficient for such a priceless artefact.

The young man approached Trevor at his desk. 'Where do you keep the Leopard Cup. Caged up in the dungeons?' The woman sniggered behind her scarf.

'It's on permanent display in Cardiff Museum,' Trevor said.

'Has it ever come home for a visit?'

'We were allowed it for a week a few years back,' Trevor said. 'They had to make a special, reinforced glass display case and sent a bodyguard who sat next to it the entire time.'

Trevor was aware of his head shaking from side to side. It was always worse when he spoke to strangers. The more he tried to control the shaking, the worse it got. He didn't bother trying any longer. He'd given up trying to shave too, so now his long beard rustled over his cardigan as though rippling in a light breeze.

'I suppose the whole town came to have a look,' the girl said.

'We had fifty more visitors than a normal week,' Trevor said. 'It would have been cheaper to have taken a coach load to Cardiff.'

The couple made appropriate noises of surprise and moved away further into the museum. They stopped outside the life-size replica of Basil Jones's general stores, with the shelves of post-war soap powder, teas, biscuits, cereals, tinned vegetables, cigarettes. Every visitor said the same thing. How they remembered their mother or grandmother having the same brands in their larders. Visitors chuckled at the out-dated advertising slogans. '*Kellogg's All-Bran – Cures Constipation*' was the one that caused the loudest laughs, in large print on the front of the packet. Trevor had spent his childhood in the cramped rooms behind that shop. Him, his two brothers, mother and grandparents. All dead and buried now, and he wouldn't be far behind them. Basil Jones had been his maternal grandfather. Trevor's father never made it off the beaches at Dunkirk. Not one of the family had ever visited his father's grave in France. He remembered the day his mother had closed the shop for the last time and the man from the museum offering her five pounds for the pre-war bacon-slicer and cash till.

The couple began reading out the names of the shops on the old High Street from the black and white photographs on the wall. Basil Jones – grocers, Bevan Evans – butchers, Aled Griffiths – chemists, Hugh Williams – ironmongers. The young man was calling out the names in a comedic Welsh accent. The English all acted out the same juvenile joke. Trevor rang the hand-bell and shouted, 'ten minutes please, ladies and gentlemen.'

The couple returned to the display cases near the door. One of the cases was devoted to tools and weapons.

'The axe-head at the back is carved from jade,' Trevor said. 'Do you know where the nearest jade to Wales could be found in those days?' he asked. 'The Alps,' Trevor said without waiting for their reply. This was one of his favourite facts.

'The ancients were trading precious minerals over thousands of miles, well before the birth of Christ,' he continued.

'Christ,' said the young man. His partner giggled.

Trevor then pointed out his three bronze axe-heads and told the story of how he found them. 'A sapling must have seeded itself below the axe-heads and grown up around them, literally raising them up out their burial place.'

'Unless someone found them and put them into a hole in the tree,' said the young man.

'No, there was no hole,' said Trevor.

The girl dropped a single pound coin into the donations box on their way out. Trevor locked the door, the keys jingling in his shaking hand, and watched the couple walk arm in arm past his window, back towards the castle exit.

'There must have been a hole,' the young man said.

A Gathering of Driftwood

Their raw, pulped feet sink into the warm sand as though into whipped cream. Tall dunes of driftwood, bleached and hard as ivory, curve in a spinal line at the high-water mark. Salted bones from ocean crossings, skeletal wooden hands grasping for a rescue. The young male picks up boomerang lengths and spins them into the returning surf. His female companion kneels and photographs the empty beach and him. The heated wind and jade green breakers hurl at the baked shore, coating a fine sea fret onto the couple's sun-reddened faces. Their voices are snatched away by the sibilant forces, up with the seabirds that hang in the air like kites.

'Look at the camera!' she yells.

'Can you believe this place?' he walks backwards for her, arms outstretched against the wind.

She frames him against the monochrome colours of sand and surf, his red t-shirt the only vibrancy against the pearl sky. In the middle distance, great black boulders lumber into the water, rollers breaking over them, exploding plumes of suds high over their massive shoulders.

Up close to one of giant rocks, he wades into the surf, his bush-hat pulled down low against the sun's last clang of the day. She packs her camera back into a shoulder bag and feels its strap scald the sunburn on her back and across her breasts. She'd been walking topless in the heat of the day. She'd never bared herself in that way before. Other men she'd paired with would have passed juvenile comment or groped her. If there had been any other trekkers she wouldn't have done it, but they hadn't seen another soul, mile after melting mile. He'd stopped and peeled off his sweat soaked t-shirt, then turned his back to her and pissed. In the time it took him to finish she'd taken off her shirt and bra and pressed them into the top of her rucksack. When he'd turned back round, he seemed not to notice. Sharp words on her tongue, dissolved.

'Come see this.' He calls to her from a boulder now encircled by seawater.

She takes small steps through the cold swell to where he stands leaning with both hands on the wall of rock.

'Look at the size of these.'

The rock bristles with thousands of mussels, plump as beef steaks, glittering black through graffiti of barnacles.

'Supper tonight. I need to wade out deeper.' He strips off, throwing his shorts and underpants to her; laughs when she screws up her nose. For a bag, he ties a knot in the bottom of his t-shirt.

She reaches again for her camera. Through the lens she watches his penis rise and fall on the lumpen sea; his buttocks appear and disappear under the waves as he reaches for the fattest shells.

When the sun was high, they'd arrived at a stream that crossed the forest track, cascading steeply into a series of pools, one of them deep enough to bathe in. They'd unloaded their rucksacks and taken handfuls of the iced water to drink, then rubbed it over their faces and mosquito bitten arms and legs. He'd sat on a rock, taken off his boots and socks then dangled in his bare feet. She'd done the same.

'Oh, fuck it.' He'd stripped naked and dived in.

There hadn't been any intimacy since they'd joined up two days ago. They'd shared food, a tent, but that's all.

'Are you coming in? It's bliss.'

She'd slipped off her shorts but not her knickers and walked into the water. She held his eye as she stepped deeper in, until the pool wetted between her legs, then she flattened out and dived under. The snowmelt stung her skin and took away her breath. She'd swum underwater to his legs then stood close to him, putting her hands on his shoulders. He'd kissed her on the lips then fallen backwards, taking her with him. She'd fought against it, the temperature had frozen her co-ordination, her legs felt awkward, she couldn't find her feet. She'd surfaced, shouted at him to stop, then waded out and pulled on her shorts. Avoiding his look, she'd found a towel in her rucksack and draped it across her shoulders and breasts. He had followed her out and dressed.

'Sorry, I didn't mean to piss you off.'

'I'm a crap swimmer that's all.'

He wades back to where the sand absorbs the waves' last ripple and passes her his red t-shirt full of mussels. She gives him his shorts in exchange.

On the dirt road that led to the beach they'd passed a general-stores. Still open, they buy wine, tobacco and things he says he needs for the supper.

In light that shines gold onto their faces and into their eyes, they collect driftwood for the stove. The great rocks are back out at sea to catch mussels. Bats lift like locust from the forest canopy to feed on insect smoke. The marbled waves peter out in sweeping flows that smooth away their footprints and bathe their toes. The sun cracks into the hot pan of sea, the yolk breaks and runs. Albumen stars spit constellations onto indigo.

The single room hostel has a handful of wooden bunks lined along the clapboard walls. A couple of worn sofas, a cupboard and a wood-burning stove make up the remaining furniture.

He poaches the molluscs in wine and cream. She lights candles, breaks bread and finds bowls and beakers in the cupboard with small drifts of sand behind the cracks in the doors. The sound and smell of the sea cascade into the darkening room, steeping the human flotsam. The scalded shellfish open and reveal their succulent hearts.

Wounded

Tim's father said he could keep the penknife. Tim found it in his father's shed, in a biscuit tin with a picture of a plough-horse on the lid. The penknife was buried like a nugget of bright silver in the dull grey of and screws and drill bits. It had a mother-of-pearl handle and a single narrow blade, sharp as paper.

'Don't tell your mother,' his father said. 'She'd never allow it.'

Tim held on to that penknife right through the summer holidays, moving his fingers over the smooth cold in his pocket. He'd cut crabbing line with it, winkled limpets off rocks, and carved his initials TGW on the apple tree.

Now he sat cross-legged on the lawn, skinning the bark off a stick. When it was done, he was going to sharpen it to a point and tape some bird feathers on the end, and when that was done, he was going to cut a stick from the hedge and make a home-made bow and arrow. The knife came up against a knot in the wood. He pressed harder. The knot lifted but the knife skidded and stabbed his thigh, disappearing up to its hilt. It wasn't bleeding and it didn't hurt.

Tim limped into the house feeling the weight of the knife pull on him, like his skin had snagged on bramble. His mother stood at the kitchen sink with her back to him. She turned and her eyes followed his arm down. She swore at him. He'd never heard his mother swear before. She put her wet hands under his arms and lifted him onto the draining board. Tears now fell heavy onto his shorts and thighs, but it still didn't hurt.

'Where the hell did you get this,' she yelled at him and put a cloth over the knife. 'Don't touch, I'll fetch Mrs Blackwell.'

Mrs Blackwell was the nurse who lived next door. She

68

and his mother weren't on speaking terms. His mother had called Mrs Blackwell's daughter 'a little tart' to her face, for sitting on our front wall and kissing a boy. Mrs Blackwell got wind of it, knocked on their door and asked his mother if she'd never been a teenager herself.

Mrs Blackwell strode into the kitchen with his mother in tow. She lifted the cloth and looked at the knife sticking from his leg.

'How long is the blade?' she asked him. She put her hand on the pearl handle.

Tim grabbed her wrist. 'No!'

'I'm not going to hurt you. How long is the blade?'

He showed her how long with his thumb and forefinger.

'Thank goodness we've got lots of fat down there,' she said. 'Hold his hands please.'

Tim's mother held his hands away. They heard the front door go. His father in from work.

Mrs Blackwell pulled out the blade with one quick 'slurp'. His flesh bulged out like the lips on his goldfish. He yelled and cried, but it still didn't hurt. The nurse dabbed at a little blood with the cloth. His father came into the kitchen. Tim's mother took the knife and jerked it in his face.

'What the hell are you thinking giving him knives? He's ten years old, you useless idiot.' She threw the knife on the floor and began to cry.

'You never do a damn thing with him, and when you do, you give him a knife,' she screamed, and ran upstairs. 'In front of Mrs Blackwell, of all people,' she yelled down.

Tim's father picked up the knife, closed the blade and put it in his pocket. He walked past his son with his head down and said sorry to the floor. Tim watched through the window as his father went into his tool shed and closed the door behind him.

Then it began to hurt.

Sculpted Bones

Robert put his two-seater through its paces on the empty roads. Wedge-shaped and low slung, it wasn't bad for someone not yet thirty. A switch on the dashboard raised up the concealed headlights, slow and disdainful, like the eyes of a waking cat. They were hungover from the night before. They'd rinsed the wine, white then red. They'd ordered large brandies over coffee then slept badly after clumsy, lazy sex. She'd wanted to sleep but let him. Both of them on their sides, drowsy, his knees inside hers, like spoons.

Mid Wales: agricultural villages and fallow towns. Pebble-dash chapels with pegboard noticeboards straddling plain memorial stones. Battered family farms, fowl scratching amongst cabbages. Edgy sheepdogs patrolling gateways. Working men's clubs with shit-spattered neon signs missing jigsaw pieces of glass. Pubs in palliative care advertising a quiz night or televised football. Nicotined windows with 'Saloon' or 'Lounge' etched in curling letters. Battened down takeaways – The Bengal Tiger, Peking House.

Robert told Naomi of the evening he'd spent in a similar country pub in Wales. The locals had broken into song – Welsh hymns. He'd tasted the strong brew of Welsh hills and valleys, coalmines, chapels and rugby clubs fermented in that pub, but then some boozed up locals had balanced a metal bucket on top of the toilet door which had booby-trapped him, cutting the bridge of his nose. The heady liquor of song had been watered down with a feeling of 'what was he doing in this shithole?'

'Sounds like you felt the falling bucket part of Welsh heritage,' Naomi said.

Naomi told Robert of her days as a trainee solicitor in a

Valleys' town. A mining community falling apart. Of living in a bedsit above a fish and chip shop. No heating. A square of cardboard taped over a hole in the bedroom window. So cold in the winter there were ice-crystals on the bedding where she'd exhaled during the night. The chip shop owner had an unerring sense of when she was going to dash from the bathroom back to her bedroom wrapped only in a towel. He'd be at the foot of the stairs, looking up.

'Didn't you give him a quick flash?' asked Robert. 'He might have reduced the rent.'

The only businesses that appeared to be open now were corner shop newsagents with meagre tokens of Christmas in the windows. Locals exiting with a newspaper and tobacco. The lottery checked for another week. The dog walked and its bowels moved.

On past visits they'd mooched in the small town antique shops that would have been called junk shops in the city; dusty mixtures of second-hand tat and an occasional find. They'd taken home a half-decent oil painting last time.

'That was an antique shop back there, wasn't it?' Robert pulled the car over.

'I'd rather find coffee,' Naomi said.

'More chance of finding a Picasso.' Robert got out of the car into the drizzle.

The painting on the earthenware statuette was crude, but the modelling of the peasant boy was lifelike. Long, sensual legs in maroon leggings. A blue ballet dancer's tunic covered a muscular torso. The blond-haired head turned arrogantly over its right shoulder and a tied bag on a stick over its left.

'He looks like a statue of a Greek God,' Naomi said. 'Adonis.'

'He's got sculpted bones, sure enough,' the antique dealer said.

The statuette stood on the floor in the back of the car like a child, wedged in with coats.

'That was a steal,' Robert said.

'Now can we find coffee?'

'Shout if you see a hotel,' said Robert. 'I don't fancy Taff's Caff.'

'Fucking English snob.' Naomi sunk down in her seat with her scarf pulled up to her nose. Closed her eyes.

Robert always felt horny after a heavy night. He looked down at Naomi's outstretched legs. He wanted to touch their litheness, like the tactile limbs of the statuette. He wanted to slide his hand up her short skirt, but he knew it wouldn't travel far. For her it was in bed only. She tended towards the strait-laced. Something he'd have to work on.

'It's not a hotel, but it'll have to do.' Robert pulled up outside a stone built cottage that had been converted to a catch-all gift shop, restaurant, ice-cream parlour, B&B.

'As long as they sell coffee,' said Naomi. A cow-bell chimed as Robert opened the door and ducked under a low lintel armoured with horse brasses. On every surface there were toby jugs, commemorative plates with 1980s' faces of the Prince of Wales and Diana, Welsh dragons made in China, dolls in black hats and tea-towel maps.

'Textbook,' Robert said.

'Just order.'

A waitress came from behind a chest freezer of ice-creams.

'We'll have two double-shot expressos, with hot skimmed milk on the side,' Robert ordered.

'Sorry, but we only do black or white normal coffee,' the waitress said.

'Two white normals it is then.'

The waitress exited through a rainfall of strung beads.

'Do you have to take the piss?' Naomi said.

'We'll both be drinking it soon.'

Robert paced the room, lifting plates and toby jugs, scanning the underside. Naomi took a compact from her bag and re-lipsticked. There was a rack of leaflets advertising things to do, places of interest. The coffees arrived. Robert took a leaflet to the table.

'Apparently the village church has the "oldest Celtic stone font in Wales", and there are Celtic carvings on the stone alter. Shall we go and say our prayers?' Robert blew on his drink.

'Will they be answered?'

'Only if you're a good girl.'

'Unlikely then.' Naomi put the compact back into her bag.

Robert waved at the waitress as though he was holding a pen, writing the tab. Naomi hated it when he did that. One down from clicking fingers.

The churchyard was semi-derelict, drowning in vegetation. Bracken, nettles and ivy had consumed all but the tallest of headstones. Many had toppled or been knocked down. Saturday night sport for bored teenagers. The cobbles in the path leading to the church door, prized apart by dock weed.

'There's something about decomposing buildings. I try to see ghosts,' Robert said. 'Not ghosts exactly, but photographs of the past. Black and white pictures of people, buried under the nettles now.'

Inside, the church had been tended to like a grave. Birthdays and sad days. Flowers in mildewed jars, weeded and dusted pews, the grass of disuse mown by the dwindling few. They ran their fingers over the stone font.

'The stonemason who carved this is buried outside. I can feel it,' Robert said. 'Gives me vertigo.'

'You might be standing on his bones.' Naomi was

73

reading the moulded handwritten requests for prayer, pinned on a cork board. 'They planted the chosen few inside.'

Robert was climbing a stone spiral staircase that went up from the nave. Narrow and unlit, his shoulders brushed both sides.

'Come and see this.'

At the top, a wooden floored platform overlooked a pit full of nothing but bird-shit and pigeon feathers. Some winged carcasses. Ribcages rising from scraps of putrefying meat. Two vertical arched slits letting in chilled winter light onto a rotting wooden frame. The bells gone.

In the dark space Robert turned, held Naomi's arms, and kissed her. She responded. Their mouths and tongues working each other's. Robert again felt the urge to put his hand up between her legs. To have sex, there, against the damp wall. Naomi ended the kiss.

'Can we get out of this bird's graveyard? It stinks.'

Back outside she led the way around the back of the church. There was a shed-sized stone vault with a gothic, scrolled iron gate just visible among the yew and holly. Blood red berries dropping on the emerald mossed slate roof. Robert pushed open the unlocked gate. On either side of the inner walls were thick stone shelves. On the shelves, decomposed wooden casks.

'Jesus, they're coffins.' Naomi backed out.

From the mire inside one of the coffins, its wooden side rotted away, the arm of a skeleton hung down. Robert viewed the arm like he'd viewed the statuette. His eyes close, moving up and down its anatomy. In the bell loft he'd felt a sexual urgency which hadn't dissipated. He felt it now, in his chest, in his shallow breathing. He felt a need to do something illicit, something carnal, to go all the way. To pull the bones into the ordure that pasted the inscribed floor.

He found Naomi back in the car. 'Can we go home now?' she said.

Robert opened a bottle of red. He put a glass into Naomi's hand and filled it. He sat on the sitting-room floor in-between her legs. The statuette stood in the fireplace without a grate, its head turned languidly across one shoulder, looking out into the room.

'It's Dick Whittington,' Naomi said. 'Streets paved with gold.'

Robert moved his hands up Naomi's thighs. 'I'll stick with sculpted bones.'

Canoe

The blacksmith's heat that hammered the Prairies had spread west that summer, bending the people like horseshoes under the clang of it. The sun's rays nailed through the forest canopy, hot and resinous, steeping the air to a green tea.

The canoe was beached on shingle, at the apex of the sea loch that brimmed westwards as far as the eye could see, emptying out into the Pacific, a day's journey away. The turquoise water was photograph still. A jeweller's alchemy of glacier blue and reflected chlorophyll from the galaxy of trees that stood high on all sides. The silence stung my ears, as though my sense of hearing had been ripped away. I shouted. I had to check that noise existed there, that sound would still travel from mouth to ears.

The naïve mountains around me said: 'We're bare as time.'

I stripped off my clothes. My nakedness seemed reciprocal and right. The only sound came from my heart and lungs, and from the gargle of water split apart by the wooden paddle and bow of the canoe.

When I'd gone far enough, I lay on the duckboards and let the canoe drift to a stop. Eagles mixed overhead on the rising thermals from the forest. The silence threatened me. I was afraid of capsizing and drowning in the vacuum, making no sound, like a toppling tree in a lifeless forest. I loaded a cartridge into the shotgun, aimed at the void and fired. The water and trees and sun absorbed the report as though a single branch had snapped in the multitude – its significance not worthy of an echo. The stillness re-encircled, left me parched of air and smothered in sky.

Profile Pictures

If I'd seen my ex-wife Sylvie on the internet dating site, I'd have pressed the unsubscribe button. I nearly unsubscribed when I saw her cousin Wendy's profile picture. I suppose seeing anyone you know on an internet dating site is embarrassing, like seeing them naked. Makes you want to shield your eyes.

Wendy and her husband David used to live in the next village to us. She's tall for a woman, close to six foot. One of those russet-faced countrywomen who prefer animals to people. Horses, dogs, cats; she'd always kept at least one of each. David was a landscape gardener with a list of well-heeled, regular clients. They moved into the adjoining county two years ago, to a larger house with a few acres of land. Enough to graze a horse for Wendy. Sylvie kept in contact with emails and the occasional morning coffee, but I haven't seen Wendy or David since they left.

Wendy looks faintly ridiculous on the dating site. She probably thinks the same about me and would've been equally embarrassed to see my own vain attempt at looking ten years younger. She's posted a long-distance profile picture of herself, sitting on a low wall next to a garden pond, wearing a summery pair of red shorts with her long legs stretched out in front of her. It would be a coquettish pose for a younger woman, but Wendy's well into her fifties. She looks uncomfortable and, at the same time, amused. That's typical of Wendy. She always saw the funny side.

Before Sylvie and I separated, Wendy and David would come to our place for supper and we'd go to theirs. On one occasion, Sylvie had been at the stove all day and, by early evening, had cooked herself into a filthy mood. She'd prepared three courses from scratch, with canapés to have with pre-dinner drinks.

'Another big production?' I said. 'Just a bowl of pasta would do. It's meant to be about the company, not the food.'

'I thought for you it's all about the drink,' Sylvie said.

Wendy had worn red that night too. A long dress with a low neckline and a split up one side revealing a bare thigh. Her chest was freckled and brown from the sun. Sylvie had never liked putting on that sort of show. She'd worn baggy black trousers and a sensible blouse.

While Sylvie clattered around with the food, David told stories of the clients' houses he visited, quoting for work. The valuable paintings hung on the walls, the ten grand sculptures on the terraces. David was one those people who knew everyone. Wendy ran her own home-visit manicure business. Between the two of them they were a smörgasbord of gossip, although they bickered like a pair of geese. Sylvie and I tended not to bicker, not in front of anyone anyway. We just curdled inside. Our office-bound lives felt mundane compared to Wendy and David's.

The more Wendy drank, the more her rough language peppered the conversation. Men she didn't like became 'fucking dickheads' and women, 'bitches on heat'. She had the deep-throated laugh of a man at a bar who'd heard a dirty joke, throwing back her head with her mouth full open. I did all I could to take my eyes off her bare leg.

Over dinner we got talking about the divorced woman who lived alone in a remote cottage between our house and Wendy and David's. At the time, she'd been the subject of village whispers.

'You know she's taken a much younger lover?' David said. 'A painter and decorator she hired to paint her window frames.'

'Who can blame her?' Wendy said, 'What woman would say no to fucking a fit young man?' Under the table, all through dessert, she'd been running her foot down my leg.

I was the only one who laughed. Sylvie started to collect up the empty dessert plates. David stared into the bottom of his wine glass.

After they'd gone, I helped Sylvie load the dishwasher and hand-wash the champagne glasses.

'Why can't you buy yourself some more feminine clothes, clothes like Wendy's?' I said. 'Make more of an effort.'

'So drunks like you can gawp at my tits?'

'I wasn't gawping at Wendy's, if that's what you mean.'

'When you weren't playing footsie with her, your eyes were popping.'

'There'll be no popping of anything with you.'

'Don't you think you've had enough to drink for one night?' she said. That's how it was between us.

By the time Wendy and David moved away the painter and decorator had stopped seeing our divorcee neighbour. I sometimes saw the woman alone on the village lanes, walking her dog. I stopped the car once and tried chatting, but she wasn't interested.

Sylvie and I stopped sleeping together. Our king-size bed wasn't wide enough for the gap we both wanted. That led to the inevitable.

I heard David left Wendy and moved in with the landlady of their local pub. I shouldn't be cynical about Wendy's attempts to look alluring on the dating website. All the women I've dated so far said they were depressed to some degree. I think they confuse depression with loneliness.

I've sent Wendy a message through the dating site, just to say 'Hi', as her cousin's ex-husband, for old time's sake.

The Composer's Tall Trees

Charles could see the composer's tall trees from the road. The dark green cumuli of their topmost branches dwarfed the shorter specimens around them. The trees were Corsican Pine, that much he did know, but he knew next to nothing about the composer. He wouldn't have been able to hum a note from a single symphony or choral piece.

He followed the signposts into the country estate's car park and reversed into a spot where he could see other cars arriving. Edwina had said she'd be driving a red Peugeot and wearing yellow trousers. She'd know him from his white Honda and khaki trousers.

I'm in the carpark, he texted.

A red car entered the car park and he watched as the female driver reversed into a slot, then re-lipsticked in the rear-view mirror. From the bottle of aftershave he kept in the glove-compartment, he sprayed generously onto his collar. Yellow trousers. It was her. Her cut-offs finished tightly at her mid-calf, revealing suntanned lower legs and, on her feet, a pair of blatantly new white trainers gleamed in the sun.

Her mostly dark hair was pulled into a ponytail with a red fabric flower on the band. She was older than the photographs on her dating profile, but then every woman he'd ever met through the internet was, and, if truth be told, he was shorter than the six foot he claimed.

'Hello, you must be Edwina. I'm Charles. Did you find it okay?' He went for the air-kiss on the cheek contact, rather than the handshake, which he always thought was more appropriate for a round of golf than a date.

'Yes, I remembered that I've been here before, a few years ago now. I brought my daughter while she was still a toddler.'

'So, you'll remember the composer's tall trees?' He stopped and pointed towards the tall group of evergreens that dominated the sky. 'Corsican pines. They inspired him to write some of his most famous works.'

'No, I'm afraid I don't remember. Mums with toddlers in pushchairs don't have time to study trees.'

In the entrance hut, the woman at the till welcomed them to the estate. Charles reached for his wallet and paid for them both. The woman gave them their receipt and a flimsy map, and hoped they'd enjoy their visit.

'I'll pay for the coffees later,' Edwina promised, as they exited into the grounds.

He opened the map. 'If we go around in an anti-clockwise direction, we'll pass the café at coffee time, and then via "Lover's Walk" to do the trees last thing before we leave. First stop – the kitchen garden with the rare "melon yard" '.

'You've obviously got things all worked out,' she said.

They told each other about their grown-up children as they walked side by side past the herbaceous borders, stopping every so often for Charles to pick a leaf, rub it between his fingers, and put it to his nose.

'I've got two,' he said, 'but to say "they keep me busy" would be an exaggeration.' He didn't see much of them. Mostly it was texts, with cards on the usual annual milestones. 'Tell me about yours.'

'I've only got one. She recently finished university with a law degree.'

She stopped to retrieve a photo of her daughter off her mobile phone. He looked at the photograph of a dark-haired, tall young woman in a graduation gown with Edwina standing next to her in an expensive looking dress and hat. 'You must be very proud of her. Education didn't suit either of mine.'

They'd reached a fork in the pathway. Left to the café, right to the walled garden. 'I love walled gardens, don't you?' he asked. 'These places make growing things look so easy.'

'I'm not interested in cultivating anything. What grows in my garden is an accident. As long as there's room for my lounger, where I can read a book. I don't even mow the lawn.'

'I could do the mowing for you.'

'My ex comes and does things like that for me.'

Charles felt vaguely uncomfortable hearing about peace treaties with ex-husbands. He felt more at home with cold wars.

'Shall we sit for a while and enjoy the sunshine?' he asked.

There was an empty bench overlooking a circular pond with a small statue of a cherub holding a plate. Water trickled from the overflowing plate onto the cherub's feet and back into the clear water.

'Just to let you know, I can only stay a couple of hours,' she said.

He threw a head of lavender into the fall of water at the cherub's feet and watched it struggle to stay afloat. 'Let's continue walking towards the café, have coffee, and then I'll show you the composer's trees.'

They rose from the bench to let a couple with a dog on a lead take their place.

'Isn't she lovely? Such sad eyes,' Edwina said to the dog's owners. She scratched the dog's ears. 'I bet deep down you're happy.'

They walked for a while in silence. Charles thought it had to be Edwina's turn to start a fresh subject.

'I'm thinking about getting a dog now my daughter is leaving home,' she said. 'I feel I need the company.'

'Aren't you looking forward to being a free agent?'

'I suppose not, otherwise I wouldn't be on a dating site.'

'A free agent to drop everything and disappear away for a weekend. To be spontaneous?'

'I could have done all that while my daughter was at uni – but didn't. Unless something has been in my diary for weeks, I try to avoid it.'

They reached the café. Housed in an old stable block, the tables inside were unoccupied, but the ones in the courtyard sunshine looked more inviting.

'Why don't you go and find us a table and I'll go inside and order.' He watched her weave between the tables and remembered that she'd offered to pay for the coffees. Too late now. He looked at the reflection of himself in the café's floor-to-ceiling window. His patch of baldness had expanded with his waistline. He pulled in his tummy. A blackboard behind the till advertised 'home-baked scones, homemade jam & whipped cream'.

As he carried the tray of coffees and scones to the table, he saw her scrolling through something on her phone. 'Have I got lots of competition?'

'Most of them turn out to be married, looking for one-night stands.'

'I assure you, I'm neither. I'm the real thing, like these scones and jam, apparently.'

'I can't tell the difference between homemade and bought in,' she said, spreading a thin layer of cream onto a skim of jam.

Charles looked over to the composer's tall trees. Their dark presence was unmissable. Although the slight breeze moved the tops of the shorter trees around them, there was a stillness and promise in the giant's shadows. He recalled reading that the composer had rented a garden cottage on the estate during periods of intense creativity, and wondered whether the cottage was still there, still available for let.

'Do you like weekend adventures?'

'With people I know very well.'

'I didn't mean…'

She concentrated on her phone and scrolled through messages. 'My daughter says she caught an earlier train.'

'You've time to visit the trees, I hope?'

They drained their cups, took last bites from the scones, and walked in silence until he asked, 'Can I hold your hand?' She put her hand into his but let go shortly afterwards when they had to move into single file to let a wheelchair pass. He advanced his hand to be re-taken then, after a few moments, retreated it to his pocket.

'Can you imagine having the patience to watch these grow?' He peered up through the basket-weave of Corsican Pine branches and pressed his fingers to the trunk of one of the tallest pines. 'I swear you can feel the beating heart of a tree if you concentrate.' She put a hand on the trunk.

'Feel anything?'

'Only some creepy-crawly walking over my fingers,' and reacted as though the tree had given her an electric shock. 'I really must be on my way.'

'I'll walk you to your car. Would you like to meet up again sometime soon?'

'Oh dear, the dreaded question.'

Charles waited while Edwina reversed out of her slot and waved as she drove out of the car park. She was too far away to see whether she waved back. Returning towards the entrance hut, he found the receipt for the tickets and held it up to the same lady behind the till.

'Back again so soon?'

'My partner had to leave early, but I haven't finished with the composer's tall trees.'

'They say if the wind's blowing in the right direction, you can hear the prelude to his final symphony.'

He retraced their steps through the rippling carpet of bluebells beneath the giant pines. A gust moved the sky of living wood above him. He stopped to listen, but rather than the trees, he heard himself. Humming. Humming the opening bars to something almost hopeful.

Blueberry Muffins

Hayley lived with her mother in three damp, square rooms above *Greasy Joe's* lorry stop, on a road that ran straight as a drainpipe out of a nondescript town, the name of which mattered only to those that lived there. Greasy Joe himself, Hayley's father, had keeled over from his lardaceous arteries when she was twelve, and her mother had been bitter about it ever since.

From a mouth like a squeezed lemon her mother would say, 'Your dad fucked off and left us nothing but this dump.'

'Dad didn't fuck off, Mum. He died.'

'Well, that was very convenient for him, wasn't it? Got him out of frying eggs for the rest of his life,' her mother would say.

Since the day her dad died, Hayley's family had enlarged, not diminished. Now she had any number of doting fathers, godfathers and uncles; the men who parked their lorries at *Greasy Joe's* for a breakfast, dinner or tea break, or even to overnight, bedding down in the cabs of their lorries in the adjacent lorry park.

'Where's my darling girl, Hayley?' they asked, and they'd give her a little doll or bag of sweets, bought from their previous lorry stop. Some of them remembered her birthday, and sent cards. 'Wiv loads-o-luv from your Uncle Charlie', or 'For my bestest girl, from your Uncle Ben'.

Some of the men drivers travelled with their wives or girlfriends, who called themselves Hayley's aunties, and treated her like their favourite niece. Some of the lorry drivers were women, piloting forty-foot rigs as good as any man.

'Better than any man,' most of them said.

'Your Auntie Julie knitted this little jumper for you on

the way down from Aberdeen,' and they'd hold it against Hayley's tiny chest as she stood beside her mother at the till.

Or, 'My girls have grown out of these things now,' and they'd hand over to Hayley's mother a bin-bag full of washed and ironed hand-me-downs.

The day Hayley left school at sixteen years old, her mother had said, 'You're on drinks. I'll do the frying,' and that was that. There was no question of a job outside of *Greasy Joe's*. That was when some of the younger male lorry drivers started to flirt with Hayley, or even suggest marriage.

'When we tie the knot, you can bring me cups of tea in bed,' they'd say. It wasn't unheard of for some of them to bring her a bunch of flowers from the previous fuel stop forecourt shop, and some of the more daring ones asked if she'd like to ride with them down to Dover and back, or even across to France on the ferry.

'And where is she going to sleep, may I ask?' her mother would chime in from the fat-spitting griddle. 'Not in your stinking cab, that's for sure. Piss off!' and she'd give them one of the rancid looks she usually reserved for cyclist customers.

Now Hayley was eighteen, her mother gave her Saturday night and Sundays off. A night and a day away from the water boiler where she made mugs of tea and coffee for twelve hours straight. The red neon *Greasy Joe's* sign pulsed into her bedroom like a bleeding heart. There were some Saturday nights, in front of her bedroom mirror, when Hayley thought she was pretty enough. She blow-dried her long silky black hair and fluttered her eyelids at herself. There were other Saturday nights when she thought she was a flat-chested bag of bones that stank of streaky bacon. Either way, her boyfriend Eddie would pick her up in his articulated truck, for the overnight haul to Basingstoke.

After three hours on the road Eddie pulled into their usual layby and Hayley ran over the carriageway for McDonald's and cokes. While she was gone, Eddie pulled the curtains across the windscreen and laid out the blankets on the single bunk behind the wheel. When she climbed back up the steps to the cab, Eddie poured two large plastic tumblers of rum and she emptied in the coke. While they ate their cheeseburgers and drank their rum and cokes, Eddie watched videos of extreme fishing. Hayley rested her head on Eddie's shoulder.
    'Well, this is nice Eddie, just you and me,' she said.
    'In Alaska, the ice-truckers catch spawning salmon for their tea,' Eddie said.
    At bedtime, they stripped off to their underwear and got under the blankets. In the past, Hayley had tried some experimentation with their love making but there wasn't sufficient headroom for anything that different. Eddie said that it seemed like a lot of huffing and puffing for nothing much anyway.
    At five in the morning Hayley woke to the cough of the truck's engine and Eddie taking a piss against the front nearside wheel. She pulled on her clothes, used the McDonald's toilets and returned with coffee and blueberry muffins.
    While Eddie supervised the unload, she redid her make-up in the sun visor mirror and never left the womb of the cab. On the return journey Hayley talked about her dream to own a café by the seaside. Eddie said that was fine by him, as long as he could go sea-fishing.
    'Maybe I could sell fresh fish from a corner of the café,' he said.
    'And I would sell my homemade blueberry muffins. My

mum could do the breakfasts and lunches. And we'd close on Mondays. Mum's dream has always been to close on Mondays.'

Late on Sunday night Eddie dropped her back outside *Greasy Joe's*.

'Same again next week' he said, without stopping the engine, or taking his hand from the wheel. Hayley leaned over and kissed him on the mouth.

Back upstairs in their damp rooms her mother lay hugging a cigarette on the sofa. She didn't say hello or take her eyes from the TV screen.

'Had a good day, Mum?'

'I changed the oil in the fryers while you've been out enjoying yourself.'

In the bathroom, Hayley opened the little rectangular box she'd bought from the chemists in the service station, while Eddie had fuelled up. She hadn't told him that she'd missed coming on for the last two months. She'd mentioned starting a family in a jokey way when they'd talked about opening a seaside café.

'It wouldn't be top of my list of things to do,' was all he'd said, so she'd turned the conversation back to blueberry muffins and his chances of catching a monster moray eel.

While the test did its work, she brushed her teeth and let her hair down, but she knew without looking that it would be positive. She'd been feeling slightly sick for days, but you can't just pull over a forty-foot articulated lorry for someone to retch into the verge. She'd pretended to be asleep and willed the feeling away. The rum and cokes would have to stop – at least for her. She wouldn't tell Eddie right away; he'd still be doing the last hundred miles up north, and then he'd have to pressure-wash the cab. She'd send him a text in the morning. And what would her mum say? Her mum always said the business couldn't afford to pay any staff, not even a part-timer.

'I've got something to tell you, Eddie', Hayley texted the next morning, ten minutes before opening at 6 am. The water had boiled, and her mother had the first packs of bacon, sausage and black pudding on the griddle.

'What?' came the reply. 'I'm on the bloody A1.'

'I'm pregnant.'

Hayley didn't receive a reply, but she knew that Eddie hated the A1, especially the stretch between Harrogate and Darlington. He'd only have thoughts for the road.

By the following Saturday, he still hadn't replied to any of her texts and phone calls, and he didn't arrive to pick her up for their normal overnight run to Basingstoke. Two weeks later she went out to Eddie's rig in the lorry park. She'd spotted it from her bedroom window.

'This is Eddie's rig,' she said to the driver.

'Not anymore, Love. He jacked in his job for a cosier number at the fishfinger factory in Berwick. It's mine now.'

Baby Joseph has dozens of grandpas and grandmas, great uncles and great aunts, who all bend down to say hello while he's lying in the pram by the till. Some bring him toy lorries for when he's older, and some knit him little woollen booties and hats.

'He's so lucky to have such a big, loving family,' they say to Hayley while she fills teapots with boiling water. 'Darling little Joe. He'll never want for anything.'

Blood and Electricity

I didn't want to go to Polytechnic without Melissa. Leaving home together meant we could share a bed.

Whilst most first year students applied for rooms in the halls of residence, Melissa and I spent weekends searching out a city centre bedsit. We had to settle for adjoining single bedrooms in a depressing 1950s' bungalow in an outlying village; the mildewed, pebble-dash walls surrounded by a gloom of over-grown firs.

Melissa found a job in a travel agency in the city, which went a long way towards paying the rent. My student grant paid the balance.

Mrs Clarke, the nicotine stained landlady of our new home wore the same every day; a splattered pink housecoat over a baggy grey tracksuit that reeked of fried food. She told us that sleeping together wasn't permitted, that a cooked breakfast and evening meal would be provided Monday to Friday, and that we could use the kitchen at the weekends.

Mrs Clarke went to bed early, so we never had long to wait before one of us crossed the hallway. In the morning we crept back to our own rooms and dressed, while she cooked a monotonous dish of bacon and eggs. She sliced an onion and fried it for her own breakfast.

'Keeps me regular,' she said.

While we ate breakfast in the funereal dining room, she ate alone in the kitchen with a fork in one hand and a cigarette in the other.

On the first day at Poly, I paired up with Jimmi Polders, a tall, blond-haired South African with orange tinted spectacles and red denim baseball boots. We were on the same course. During the morning break, in the Students' Union bar, Jimmi selected Bob Marley and The Wailers on the jukebox and cock-strutted around the pool-table while

91

expertly potting balls. On the drive to a pub for a lunchtime pint, Jimmi handed me puffs of his joint. He told me he'd been thrown out of his last college for dealing.

In the second week there was a fresher's disco. I left Melissa watching the portable television in her bedroom.

'The whole year group is going. I don't want to be the odd man out,' I said. The truth was that Jimmi had talked me into it.

We met in a pub close to uni. We bought pints and played pool. Jimmi was already high.

'How's it going to work with little wifey at home?' he asked.

'How's what going to work?'

'How will you manage your fair share of screws? I can't do all the work.' Jimmi potted a stripe ball.

I thought of Melissa back in the bungalow. I'd never slept with anyone but her. I'd already heard the stories from the halls of residence. Me and Melissa would've been going to bed when the parties were just warming up.

'We can't let that happen, can we?' I said.

'Good man.' Jimmi potted another ball.

The disco was blacked out, students crammed against each other, some dancing, most just screaming at each other above the shaking noise. Tobacco and cannabis smoke mixed in the coloured lights from the stage; pink, green, strobing white. The floor was swilling with beer and drunks falling in sweat-stained mauls. Girls swayed to the music alone or in huddled groups. The bar was ten-deep with blokes waving plastic pint pots.

'Fuck this. Let's go to the SU bar. At least we'll be able to get a drink,' Jimmi shouted.

The SU bar was over-lit with white strip lights. All the sofas, chairs and most of the floor was taken.

'You get the drinks, I'll find some girls,' Jimmi said.

Balancing pints, I scanned the room. Jimmi waved from

a sofa – one of four, squared around a low table, thick with empty glasses and full ashtrays. Four girls on the same sofa as Jimmi waved too. I swore into my plastic glass.

The girls were psychology students, or sociology. An 'ology' I immediately forgot.

'Are you a rich boy, too?' one of them asked.

I looked at Jimmi. He had a girl either side of him, sharing a half-bottle of vodka. His Afrikaner looks stood out from the masses of squat Anglo-Saxons all around him. Passing males and females alike smiled at him, as though they knew him. Some lifted their glasses to Jimmi's t-shirt that read 'Ban Apartheid' and 'Free Nelson Mandela'. As his pool-table partner, I felt noticed.

'I don't like being pigeon-holed,' I said to the girl.

'Let's dance, Pigeon, while I can still walk,' she said.

On the dance floor, we pulled each other close. She pressed her tight denim crotch onto my thigh. I pressed my vodka lips onto hers.

Back in her halls of residence bedroom she pushed me onto the bed, stood over me and stripped to her bra and knickers.

'I can't do it tonight. I'm off games,' she said.

'Off what?'

'Games. I'm off games. Didn't you have girls at your school?'

'No,' I said. 'Not girls.'

She sprung me from my underpants and started doing something Melissa never had.

'She was the worst looker in the room,' Jimmi said. 'You must have been pissed.'

'Arse-holed,' I said.

In the run up to Christmas, lectures were short and irreverent. Hangovers soured the thirst for knowledge. Students wore their Christmas colours; over-long red scarves, reindeer antlers and Christmas tree earrings. There were over-the-top decorations in the halls of residence bedrooms, while nihilistic students made an ostentatious show of having none. In the SU bar, Christmas pop songs were on continuous loop. Me and Jimmi were playing pool and drinking pints.

'You're coming out tonight Si, aren't you? It's obligatory,' he said. 'We're going to get shit-faced.'

'You're shit-faced every night.'

Jimmi laughed at himself. 'Yeah, well tonight is special. It's Christmas. You might get lucky again.'

'Where shall I meet you?'

'The Oranges and Lemons.' Jimmi downed his pint.

'That's a shit-hole, isn't it?'

'It is, and there's some great bands playing there tonight,' Jimmi said.

Back at the bungalow I found a letter on my pillow with Melissa's handwriting on the envelope.

Darling, I resigned last week, but couldn't tell you. Sorry, but I hate it here. After Christmas at Mummy and Daddy's, I'm going to Australia for a few months, staying with an old school friend. After that I don't know.

Mrs Clarke put her head around the door.

'Your girlfriend packed up and moved out at lunchtime,' she cackled. 'You'll be sleeping on your own for once.'

I could hear and feel The Oranges and Lemons before I saw it; guitar bass vibrating through the city paving stones. In sight, the frosted windows flashed colours of blood and electricity. There were drinkers out in the street despite the cold; a tribe I didn't recognise. Sort of skin-heads, with face-paint and piercings. Hair spiked, shaved and dyed.

Chains snaking off military uniforms, black mainly, but some tartan and acids. Gaping vests exposed bra-less, erect nipples on liquorice lipsticked girls in shredded stockings.

Jimmi and his posse of halls-mates sat behind pint glasses and a half empty bottle of Jack Daniels.

'Si! We're doing chasers.' Jimmi pushed a glass of each in front of me. One of his entourage passed me a joint.

'What the fuck are these people? I said.

'Punk rockers. Punks. Where've you been hiding?'

The lights in the pub went out. The DJ silenced the decks. Someone made an announcement. Jimmi got out of his chair.

'Come and see this, Si,' he said.

I followed him through to the main bar. The floor was bare planks, the walls were stripped to the plaster. The stage consisted of black painted wooden blocks under raw white lights. The *Fatal Microbes* began regurgitating words into the mics. The crowd boiled into each other, skittled over by cannonballs of sound from screeching guitars. After the first number the singer pulled his cock out of his leather jeans. A roll of toilet paper landed on the stage. He pissed onto the toilet roll, then threw it unravelling, wet into the crowd. Some in the crowd responded with lit fireworks, arching them onto the stage. Bouncers moved in, crashing the firework throwers to the floor. The fireworks exploded on stage – the music didn't stop. Jimmi handed me a small brown medicine bottle with a cork.

'Breathe it up your nose,' he said.

'What does it do?'

'It'll make you come in your fucked up English head.'

I took the cork from the bottle, put it to a nostril and breathed in. I started to laugh. My face felt like it was going to split open, then my bowels and my balls. My lungs felt full of air yet empty of air.

The punk rocker's cock was still exposed. He took the string of flashing red Christmas lights from around the mic stand, pulled back his foreskin, inserted a bulb then covered it with his flesh. The music smashed into silence. He stood arms outstretched, head down, his cock flashing veiny red.

'It's an education,' Jimmi said.

Canada

You collected me from the jetty in the small logging town. I'd been waiting in a striptease bar, the lumberjack customers more interested in their beers and televised ice-hockey than the girls. I'd seen your boat from a mile out, cutting a quick white swathe through the lake. During the ride back into the forest wilderness you told me about your husband. How he hadn't got long on this Earth, how he'd been a professor of English in love with William Shakespeare, how he'd built your farm with his own two hands. I'd lied on the application form and said that I was experienced in farm work and told you I loved Shakespeare too. I watched your face as you steered the boat. Weathered, freckled, twice my age, beautiful.

Every evening the two of us raised your husband from his downstairs bed and sat him at the dinner table, your young son looking on. The four of us held hands around the table whilst he said your Quaker prayers or croaked through 'All Creatures of our God and King'. You and I sat next to each other, in our given places. I felt your fingers move in my hands, the slight compressions when he coughed, when he faltered. You held my hand a second longer after he said Amen. After dinner, we assisted him back to his bed where I'd read Shakespeare sonnets. I sensed you listening in whilst you cleared the table. Sometimes you'd sit next to me on the bed and dab a napkin to his eyes.

This photograph of the barn is the only thing I have left. The angry geese and the scurrying goats on the lush forest grass. You showed me how to milk the nannies. Slowly pinch and stroke their teats, squirting the pungent milk into the chipped enamel bowls, your teaching hands on mine.

When the kid goats started being taken at night, one by one, you said 'cougar' and asked if I'd ever shot a rifle. You wanted me to sleep and keep guard in the hayloft, said the geese would be my alarm. After supper you led me to the gun-safe in your bedroom, showed me how to load. Your eyes followed my gaze to the un-slept in side of the bed. You brought hot coffee and blankets to the barn. Sat next to me on the hay and rolled my cigarettes.

It was inevitable I should leave, leave you with a dying man and a boy. You drove me in the tractor to the boat. The heat that day was intense. You stripped off to your pants and dived in. I followed in naked. We held each other in the freezing water, and you cried.

You wrote to me a few weeks after I'd returned to England. Told me the exact time of day your husband stopped breathing.

The Beautiful Couple

'Any spare change?' The same three words the guy sitting by the stack of supermarket baskets asks of everyone. His question was directed at the beautiful couple I'd seen in my rear-view mirror as I pulled into the supermarket carpark. I'd glimpsed them alighting from a sleek BMW. Him from behind the wheel, her from the passenger side. They looked too young to be in such an expensive executive model. I thought they might be brother and sister who'd borrowed their parents' car for a shopping trip.

Both were extraordinarily tall. He was a head over six foot and she only slightly less. Both had the same lustrous, dark brown hair – almost black. His cut smartly onto the top of his ears and collar, hers cascading onto her flawless bare shoulders. Their similar shaped, perfectly proportioned faces were tanned, as though recently returned from a foreign holiday. They exuded the lithe grace of a pair of leopards, fluid and languorous in the way they moved. Adjusting my preconceptions of siblings, I trailed them as they kissed and walked hand-in-hand towards the sliding doors.

'Oh, aren't you gorgeous?' The girl stopped and crouched down to stroke the down-and-out's dog. 'What's his name?' Her other hand, still holding onto her boyfriend's, was now above her head, not letting him go. She was wearing a short, floaty summer dress with shoulder straps, in a soft red with clusters of small yellow flowers. The late April weather had been unseasonably cold but, although she appeared under-dressed, she seemed impervious to the chill wind. Her athletic, long brown legs attracted their own climate. The air surrounding the couple felt warmer and sunlit.

The seated beggar, huddled in his filthy overcoat and unravelling balaclava, didn't answer her. His eyes never wavered from the middle distance – his gaze fixated on the dour war memorial in the railed enclosure over the busy road, as though he was listening to the mildewed stone eulogise the dead.

'Any spare change, mate?' He held out his hand to me. I'd driven to the supermarket to buy a bottle of whisky, although I usually disguised my early evening shopping trips as the pressing need of something wholesome – milk or bread or a tin of soup. The cold and wet Sunday had drooped across my face, and my wife's, like a mild stroke. Alcohol was my fellow passenger over the tedious hours before bed.

'The dog's name is Jelly,' I said to the girl, as I yanked a plastic basket from the stack. This is where he spends most of his sad life.'

The young man handed Jelly's owner a two-pound coin. His long, elegant fingers were of a different species to the nicotine and ash-coloured claws of the seated man. 'Hello, divine little Jelly,' the girl said, ruffling the impassive animal's ears. 'My name's M…' She looked through the face-hole in the man's balaclava as she said her name, expecting a response. None came.

I ignored the beggar's requests for change. I'd once joked with him that he needed to invest in a contactless credit card reader. 'No-one carries "spare change" nowadays,' I said. 'Even your line of work has to modernise.'

Inside the supermarket, I dawdled by the fresh fruit and vegetables to watch the beautiful couple make their entry. I could see them through the glass sliding doors, still close to the man and his dog, the girl still squatting, her golden knees inches from the haggard face. I picked up some half-priced, wrinkled mushrooms to eat later, on a slice of toast. I pretended to look up and down the free-standing display of discounted wines and hovered a hand over some short-dated ham.

When the couple entered through the sliding doors, they were wearing matching Covid facemasks. I was sure, underneath the masks, their teeth would shine as white as their eyes and their lips ready for the next sweet taste of each other. She began picking items off the shelves and from the chillers. Her boyfriend held their basket with one hand and held her free hand with his other. I'd never before seen the mechanics of shopping while holding hands. They communicated preferences through little squeezes and tugs. I tried to deduce what they would cook and imagined the décor or their kitchen. I pictured them preparing the ingredients together, listening to music they both loved. He would chop the fresh parsley and open the wine while she grilled the fish and set two places. They might break off from cooking to slow-dance around the island unit. They'd have urgent sex wherever the need arose.

I followed my angel fish as they swam through the aisles, the drabber fish parting in respectful shoals. They bought fresh pasta and extra virgin olive oil, organic coffee beans and new season's asparagus. By the time they reached the checkout, I'd replaced my wrinkled mushrooms and short-dated ham with some fresh sardines and soda bread for my evening slice of toast. I spent more than I normally would on a bottle of wine.

I stood behind them as their purchases were scanned through. The young man said something through his facemask to the grey-haired woman on the till and she blushed and giggled. The girl turned to me and spoke. 'Isn't Jelly just adorable?'

'Cruelty, keeping a dog in those conditions,' I said. She turned away from me and put her hand on her boyfriend's waist.

The couple stopped again by the beggar and unpacked a bag of shopping. Sandwiches, chocolate, and a pint of milk for the man. A packet of dog biscuits for the animal.

'A little something for you, Carl, and some treats for Jelly,' the girl said. 'Take care, both of you,' and she kissed the dog on the top of its head. I'd never before heard anyone know, or use, the beggar's name.

'Bless you.' And I'd never before heard the man say anything other than 'any spare change?'

I kept some coins in my car for whenever I needed to feed a parking meter. I collected them up and returned to Carl and Jelly. 'There you go, Carl,' I said and tipped the coins into the tin at his feet and rubbed Jelly's ears. He didn't reply; his gaze was fixated on the couple's car as it wended its way from the carpark. The beautiful girl waved at him. I waved back a proxy hand.

Inside the supermarket, the customers at the checkouts were engaging the till-staff in friendly conversation. The supermarket trolley attendant was picking up litter by the door. A man approached me and asked if I'd like my car washed. I said yes, and that I'd wait with my friends Carl and Jelly.

Salesman of the Week

Roger had enjoyed a good year at TV-EZEE. He'd sold more new television sets than any of the other salesmen and smashed his target. He'd doubled his basic salary with commission. When any prospective customers stepped foot into the shop, his boss Conrad invariably gave Roger the first nod. Conrad had upgraded Roger's discounted staff TV to a twenty-six inch and had invited Roger and his wife Joan to his house for dinner. None of the other salesmen had ever been to Conrad's for dinner. Joan had bought a new dress and shoes.

On a Friday afternoon, after they'd locked the shop doors, Conrad kept the tradition of inviting the 'Salesman of the Week' into his office. He'd pour two large whiskies and offer up the box of cigars he kept on his mahogany desk. The desk had belonged to Conrad's father. There was a framed black and white photograph on the desk of Conrad's father shaking hands with their first customer to purchase a colour set.

This evening was Roger's sixth Friday evening in a row to be invited into Conrad's office.

'You've had an astounding year, Roger,' Conrad said. 'Everyone at TV-EZEE is proud of you.' Conrad locked the whisky bottle back into his cash safe.

'You deserve your fortnight's break. Where are you taking the family?' Conrad raised his glass to Roger's. 'Somewhere that befits a top television salesman, I hope.'

Roger chinked his glass with his boss's. 'I'm taking them to France on the ferry. Booked a caravan. Close to the beach for Joan and the little ones, and close enough to the estuary for me and our eldest to go fishing. Never been abroad before. Can't wait.'

'That's great, Roger. Cheap wine, sunshine, frogs' legs. You'll love it.'

Roger drove slowly towards home. He had the windows

down to clear his head and blow the smell of cigars off his jacket. Joan hated the smell of tobacco. He turned off his normal route and took the short detour towards the boatyard on the canal. He'd read in the local newspaper that the boatyard was selling fibreglass dinghies.

The dinghies were lined up in a row outside the chandlery, among the rusting hulls of narrowboats jacked-up on railway sleepers, and empty boat-trailers with flat tyres. There was only one colour available – pure white, with squared off bows, like bathroom soap-dishes. On a steel frame next to the new boats, hung a dozen or so outboard engines, their shiny propellers glinting in the evening sun like golden flowers. On a wooden pallet, new car roof-racks were piled neatly on top of each other.

Roger was used to doing deals. He wrote a cheque for one of each; dinghy, engine and roof-rack. He'd negotiated a two-gallon petrol tank and canvas dinghy cover, thrown in for free. Two month's commission worth, but wasn't that what he worked his balls off for? The owner of the boatyard helped Roger fit the roof-rack and rope on the dinghy.

'Bon Voyage,' the owner said as Roger drove off.

'Five hundred pounds though, Roger!' said Joan. Roger's wife, his eldest son Sammy and the two young ones stood in the drive looking up at the boat on the roof-rack. 'That's almost as much as the holiday.'

'This is what I work so hard for, Joan,' Roger said. 'Little luxuries.'

'We can barely afford the mortgage, Roger.'

'You like it though, don't you, Sammy?' Roger said to his son. 'We're going to follow the fish in this.' Roger patted the boat's side as though it was a horse.

Roger and Joan loaded the car in silence. During the day Joan had filled the suitcases and put together boxes of food. She'd borrowed a cool-box for butter, milk and bacon.

Roger shook his head as Joan brought out each box. 'Couldn't we have bought these things when we got there?' he said. 'There's a shop on the site.'

'We have no idea what they sell. I don't want to go shopping the minute we arrive.'

When the last box went in, Joan went to bed. They had to be up before dawn to drive to the south coast to catch the ferry. Roger sat downstairs with a bottle of whisky. They had overstretched a little with the mortgage. He'd just have to sell even more televisions when they got back.

The ferry crossing from Plymouth had been rough. The upper decks had been lined with passengers being ill over the side, and the toilet cubicles awash with it. Roger had brought up all his full English breakfast – it hadn't settled well on the previous night's alcohol. Joan had done the driving from home to the port while he slept it off. The weather had delayed the ferry's departure and now they had another three hour drive ahead of them in France, in the gathering gloom, on the wrong side of the road. Joan had never got the hang of road-maps.

'I've written down a list of all the road numbers and the towns to head for,' Roger said. 'It should be like joining the dots.'

They found the caravan site after five hours in the car. Roger and Joan had rowed over the route. He'd snatched his list from her lap and stopped every twenty minutes to compare his notes with a road-map of France. At one point Roger had stopped the car and slapped the legs of the young ones and told them to go back to sleep. Joan had wept.

'Why couldn't we have just gone to Cornwall?' she said.

'Because we always go to fucking Cornwall.'

Joan had looked at Roger, aghast at his language. She'd wept some more.

They woke the next morning to bright sunshine illuminating the caravan's thin, flowery curtains. Roger stretched up from their narrow double bed and opened a window. Scents of the sea and the French pine forest came in through the window. Roger thought he could smell freshly baked bread wafting from the camp-shop. The trees were ringing with bird-song, and he noticed the new dinghy's hull was covered in explosions of bird-shit. First job would be to get the boat on the water. No, maybe the first job would be to make things right with Joan. Roger moved his hand under her nightie and up between her legs. He used to wake Joan like this before they were married, before they had kids. He could sense she was awake even though her back was still turned. She began to move her body over his fingers. Everything was going to be ok.

While his wife cooked bacon, Roger walked the children to the camp shop. He bought baguettes for a picnic and croissants for breakfast. The bread was still warm and the day was getting warmer. He saw that the car parked outside the next-door caravan was from England. A man was unloading its boot.

'Good to see other Brits on the site,' Roger said. 'Looks like we're neighbours.'

'You won't meet anyone *but* Brits on this site,' the man said. 'They keep us away from the foreigners. Suits me fine. I'm Tony.'

'I've got a big favour to ask, Tony' said Roger. 'Could you help me down to the estuary with the boat?' Roger pointed at the dinghy still on the roof of his car. 'Only the lad's not big enough yet.' He ruffled Sammy's hair.

Roger had forgotten how heavy the dinghy was. Trying to manhandle the boat off the roof-rack single-handed, he'd

106

let it slip. The boat had fallen to the ground, leaving a gouge in his car's paintwork.

Roger and Tony dropped the dinghy onto the opaque green water of the estuary. Roger tied the craft to the wooden jetty, thanked Tony and promised to buy him a beer. They began the long climb back up through the forest to the caravans. Roger still needed the engine and the fishing tackle before they could fish.

'You're going fishing now?' Joan said. 'On the first morning of the first day.'

'That's the plan.'

'What about the young ones? They're dying to go to the beach.'

'Sammy's dying to go fishing, aren't you Sammy?'

They took the car the two miles to the beach. Roger helped his wife carry a beach bag, a rug, a picnic and beach toys to a spot by some rock-pools.

'We'll be back in a couple of hours,' Roger said. 'I just want to catch a fish for him from our new boat. He's too old for sandcastles.'

'Ten is not too old for sandcastles, Roger. Not too old to play with his younger brother and sister. Not too old to spend time with the whole family on the first day of the holiday.'

'Let me do this, Joan.' Roger kissed his wife on the lips.

Roger and Sammy motored up and down the estuary for three hours, until the petrol tank was almost empty. Roger had bought brightly coloured spinners from a tackle-shop back home. The fish-shaped spinners glinted in the water as they towed them. After an hour, Sammy had stopped talking about the types of fish they would catch. They'd stopped the boat and changed spinners, from silver-coloured ones to gold, from gold to red. They'd motored along at top speed, so the spinners span near the surface, and they'd gone along dead slow, so the spinners sank to the bottom. One had caught on submerged seaweed and Roger had to cut the line. After two hours, Sammy had rested his rod on the deck of the dinghy and sat opening and closing his penknife. In his mind, Roger prayed for a fish to take back to Joan on the beach.

'It's the tide, Sammy. It's on its way out. The fish are all back at sea,' Roger said. 'We'll come back tonight when the tide's turned. The fish come in to feed.'

'Can we go to the beach now?' Sammy said.

On the way, they stopped in the small town. Roger topped up the portable tank with petrol and bought some frozen sand-eels. They'd use real bait that night. Roger also bought a small, portable barbecue. He'd set it up on the banks of the estuary for when they caught.

'You said you'd be two hours,' Joan said. 'You've been gone for four.'

'Lost track of time enjoying ourselves.'

'Catch anything?'

'Tide was against us.'

'Isn't that what the boat's for?' Joan said. 'To follow the fish. That's what you said.'

Roger took a towel from the beach-bag and laid it out in the shade of the cliffs. He lay down and closed his eyes.

'You're not going to sleep now?' Joan said. 'The kids have been waiting for you to go in the sea.'

'I'm tired Joan. Try walking up and down that forest path to the estuary, twice, with heavy weights.'

When Roger woke from his nap, he was alone. He looked down to where the waves were breaking onto the sand but couldn't see his family. He stood and scanned the mile long beach as it curved around the bay and disappeared into the haze of sea and summer. He could make out Joan's vivid yellow t-shirt and the three shorter shapes of children. Joan had always liked taking the children on long walks along the water's edge with their buckets. They'd return with a collection of smooth stones, shells, crab-claws and sometimes some small live creatures from the rock-pools. Roger saw that the tide had turned. He began packing up the towels, rugs, chairs, beach bag and made a couple of trips to the car. When he returned to the beach, he saw that Joan and children were halfway back. He set off to meet them.

'We're going back to the caravan now,' he said to the young ones. 'Sammy and me are going fishing again.'

'We're not going back, Roger,' Joan said. 'You've done your fishing. Now spend time with your other children, with the family.'

'I have to catch a fish, Joan. For Sammy's sake.'

When Joan saw that Roger had packed everything up, she demanded that he gave her the car keys.

'I'll get it all back out again,' she said.

'Don't be like that, Joan. We have the rest of the holiday to come to the beach.'

Joan held her hand out for the keys. Roger didn't hand them over.

Back in the beach car park, while Roger was closing the boot, his wife leaned over to the ignition, extracted the keys and threw them into the long dune grass. Roger didn't see the keys fly through the air and didn't see where they landed.

In the time it took for Joan to tell Roger what she'd done with the car keys, she'd unloaded her children and walked them to the ice-cream kiosk over the road. While Roger was still on his hands and knees in the dune grass, Joan walked the children back with their ice-creams, took the rug from the boot of the car, spread it out in the dunes and sat and ate the ice-creams. By the time Roger had enlisted the help of passers-by in the search, Joan had started a game of French cricket on the sands. By the time they returned to the caravan, the tide in the estuary was almost at its highest. Roger and Joan hadn't spoken. The children too had been silent. They were getting used to the long periods when their mother watched the passing roadside with her head turned to the side-window, when their father drove too fast and swore under his breath.

Roger and Sammy hooked the thawed-out sand-eels onto the spinners and zig-zagged their way several times up and down the estuary. Roger reconfigured the rods to take floats and they sat becalmed, drifting with the tide, his eyes fixed on the fluorescent colours as the floats bobbed in the breeze.

'Maybe we'll have more luck with crabs,' Sammy said.

There were tears in Sammy's eyes. The boy was like his mother. Over-emotional.

'You can go crabbing from the jetty with the young ones. I thought you wanted to do the grown-up stuff?'

'There were more fish in Cornwall.' Sammy said.

Roger tied the dinghy back to the jetty in darkness. There was a new chill in the air and clouds gathered out towards the sea. Roger remembered fishing as a boy with his own father. They'd always pulled them out, one after another. He remembered his mother sitting on the rocks with them with a picnic basket, taking photographs of him holding the mackerel his father would cook over a primus stove back at their tent.

'You have to be patient with fishing,' Roger said.

'Perhaps if we have a day on the beach tomorrow, the fish will come back,' the boy said.

Back on the caravan steps, Joan took the boy's hand and led him inside without a word.

Roger went to his end of the caravan and found the whisky he'd bought duty-free on the ferry.

'Don't wait up for me,' he said to Joan. He'd heard that fish like to feed at night, when the weather was about to break.

Under the Paint

The hot weather was due to break that evening. I'd stowed away the mattress from the garden chair in the shed and was walking up the path to the house when I heard a 'Hello'.

Gabrielle was around forty-five, I guess. Her hair was a greying, frizzy auburn, scraped back into a thick tail. The appley skin of her cheeks belied her years. She was unmarried, lived next door with her elderly folks in the same old pile she'd been born into. I'd never known her do a full day's work. She did an hour here and there at the village school, listening to the young kids read, but that was voluntary. I'd often see her early evening, sat at an outside table at the village pub, smoking a cigarette and drinking a small wine. All the locals knew her, but no-one ever seemed to keep her company. She spoke to people as though she was talking to a kitten, petting and fussing it, whispered and wheedling. Her watery eyes focused on your right ear rather than directly at you and her smile looked pinned on like a brooch. I'd heard talk that she'd been raped in her twenties and it had stayed in her head.

I'd flirted with her once. When I was a still a village newcomer, she'd come around late one evening to 'borrow' a cigarette. She was wearing bright pink lipstick and overly dark mascara. I'd poured her a glass of wine and lit her smoke from a candle. After the second glass she'd taken off her shoes. She wore a fine gold band on one toe. I said I couldn't believe she was still single. It was a stupid line I regretted. I said that and other stuff, then backed off. I'd pressed around the edges and sensed vulnerability, like finding rot in the window frames, under the paint.

'Hi, Gabrielle.' She'd been knocking on the door. Her usual pinned-on smile was missing.

'Is everything alright with your spring water?' she said, straight in.

I wasn't sure I'd heard her correctly. She was looking at the old standing tap that stuck three feet up from one of my overgrown borders. Before the mains water arrived, the village had relied on underground springs. When I'd first bought the cottage, a dribble came out of the tap, but only after heavy rain.

'My spring water?' I walked to the tap and turned. Nothing. 'Hasn't worked since I moved in,' I said.

'Only I was walking in the woods this afternoon and saw the spring gushing from the ground,' she said.

'Gushing?'

'And our fountain has stopped working,' she said.

In the front lawn of her folks' place was a small ornamental pond with a fountain. It wasn't much more than a single lead pipe that spurted irregular amounts. Her father had once told me that it was spring fed.

'My mother and father are away you see,' she said.

I told her that I'd walk up to the woods after my supper. I wanted to see this 'gushing from the ground'.

'I'm not sure there'll be much I can do,' I said.

'Thank you anyway,' she said in that wheedling voice of hers and walked back next door. I'd expected her to say she'd come along.

After I'd eaten, I went up to the small spring fed pump in the woods. Gabrielle's parent's shabby manor house and my pokey gardener's cottage both gold-framed in the evening sun. The machinery inside the crumbling brick pump-house was a rusted tangle of broken pipes buried in nettles and bracken. The 'gushing' turned out to be no more than a steady trickle coming from somewhere inside the workings. I guessed an underground pipe had silted up and burst.

On my way back down over the field I'd made up my mind to invite Gabrielle in and open a bottle of wine. Perhaps I'd felt sorry for her alone in the large house. Perhaps I'd felt more than that.

I knocked on the back door. I knew it opened into their kitchen. That was where she and her folks lived most of the time, they and the two dogs sitting on sofas around a wood stove. The dogs kicked off as they always did, yelping like they'd smelt a fox. After a while I knocked for a second time. There was no possibility she couldn't have heard the barking. I reckoned she'd walked up to the pub for her lonely drink, although leaving the dogs wasn't like her.

I walked around to the front and looked at the fountain. She'd been right about that. Dry. When I glanced up at the bedroom windows Gabrielle was standing motionless in one of them. I waved at her. She didn't wave back or even look down. She just stood there watching the wind thrash the treetops and storm clouds roister over the distant hills.

A Girl like Shirley

My head aches and my mouth tastes of sex. November wind and rain slamming the bedroom window like a carwash, sky like mushroom soup. Sodden leaves from the roadside lime trees floating like jellyfish, then beaching themselves on windows or cars in the resident's parking two floors below. I listen to the traffic. The dismal shush, shush of tyres through water. I hear morning television in the sitting room next to my bedroom. Bursts of pop music, the presenter's inane laughter, and commercials. My flatmate Rhys has surfaced. No alarm clocks on a Saturday.

Asleep beside me in bed, there's a naked girl, her fleecy blond hair squashed flat between her cheek and the pillow. On the other side her hair is mussed up into the cold, damp air, soft as thistle down. I touch gently onto it like a child feeling his mother's ball of wool. Springy, bed-warm. Her sooty eye-shadow and plum lipstick smudged, last night's sweet breath gone sour. I look at the inverted nipple she's so sensitive about. It turns inwards like a small boy's. She won't let me try to suck it out. I don't know why she's so uptight about it, it's only a nipple. I think about trying to suck it out whilst she's sleeping but don't want to wake her.

I find my gown and open the bedroom door into the sitting room. Rhys has lit the mobile gas heater and moved it as close to his chair as possible without the flames singeing the fabric. The condensation from the gas has soaked the inside of the thin sash-windows. Over the back of a dining chair Rhys has hung a pair of newly-washed jeans that steam from the heat. He's warming both hands around a mug of tea. Like me, he's in a gown with the addition of a pair of ski-socks. Rhys is in the process of moving out. He and his girlfriend Shirley have been shifting boxes and bits of furniture for the last three weekends. They've bought a flat together, right across the road. I can see it from the window, over the lines of cars stopping and starting at the traffic lights.

'Final push today?' I ask.

'What the fuck happened?' he answers. He jerks his thumb over his shoulder at the table pushed against the wall. There are dirty plates, burnt down candles on congealed wax plinths, broken wine glasses. All have been swept aside in a heap. On the floor – a smashed wooden chair, both its rear legs broken. 'Was someone taken hostage?'

I don't recall how the chair was broken. A volume of drink had been taken, judging by the empty bottles on the carpet and the opened bottle of brandy. I guess I mounted the chair somehow, searching for purchase between Teresa's legs. She has a thing about tables. Earlier, she'd sashayed into the kitchen where I was preparing a Chinese. She wanted to show me her new mini skirt. We started kissing. My hands wandered up underneath – she has a habit of going without knickers around the flat. We did it on the kitchen table amongst the spring onions and chopped ginger.

'I should be gone by tonight,' Rhys says.

Down the hallway I can hear Shirley's hair-dryer. They both take a lot of time over hair. She'll come out of Rhys's bedroom looking like Audrey Hepburn in *Breakfast at Tiffany's*. That's why I don't want to wake Teresa till Shirley's gone. Teresa will look like she's been doing it on the tables.

I slouch into the kitchen and drop a teabag into a stained mug. There's a small window overlooking the shared patch of grass where residents take their dogs to shit. Over the high brick wall there's a row of horse-chestnuts lining the side-road. Two boys are collecting conkers, oblivious to the rain, their bikes laid on the grass verge. Rhys and I did the

116

same thing once. We lived close to each other on the same housing estate, have known each other since infant school. I went to college, he to university, but we're together again now. Rhys is the one with the brains and ironed shirts.

Teresa appears at the entrance to the kitchen. She leans her shoulder against the doorframe, crosses her bare legs at the knee. She's wearing one of my shirts and I see the outline of a bra. That nipple thing again. She's naked from the waist down. She wouldn't have cared about walking past Rhys. I consider asking her to go put on some knickers. Rhys has seen Teresa like this before but I don't know how Shirley will react. But then Shirley won't be here for much longer. Nor Rhys. After two years of sharing. No Rhys.

During the week when there's no Shirley or Teresa, Rhys and I go out on the town. Some weeks we go to a nightclub every night. We've brought girls back. Or rather Rhys has brought two girls back, one for each of us. He's good at making girls laugh. He says I need to lighten up. In the evening I get home before Rhys and cook us a meal even though Rhys says I can't cook. We tell each other the stories of the night before and swear we're going to have a night in playing backgammon, until it gets to around ten o clock and the pubs will soon be closing, and we say 'fuck it', put on clean shirts and jump in the car.

When Rhys told me he was going, I said, 'So what are you going to do every night? Stay in and watch television like marrieds?'

'Fuck off. Nothing changes. Shirley comes out with us that's all,' he said.

I lead Teresa by the hand back to my bedroom. I didn't think I'd want more of her this morning. We step over the broken chair and bottles on the carpet.

'I'll let you keep the table and chairs,' Rhys says.

'Don't go without saying goodbye,' I say.

'I'm only over the road for fuck's sake,' Rhys says. 'Wave at me from your bed.'

I wake to a soft knocking on my bedroom door. My watch says mid-afternoon and already the light outside is fading. The air is cold and animal; lizards in a tank.

'We're off, mate.' It's Rhys, trying to whisper.

I wrap on a gown, open the door. Rhys is there with his hand outstretched, Shirley behind him, her face made up like a water-colour painting. Teresa daubs it on in oils. I shake Rhys's hand. Shirley pecks me on the cheek but I won't have a kiss mark. Shirley doesn't leave kiss marks.

'You're only going over the road,' I say.

'Come see us if ever you get out of bed,' he says.

After I heard Rhys's car pull out of the carpark, I walk into Rhys's bedroom. Shirley has vacuumed and left a white plastic air-freshener in the corner. On the one remaining piece of furniture Rhys has left me his backgammon set with a note that that says 'Enjoy'. On the wall behind where Rhys's double bed was, there's a large damp patch in the wallpaper the shape of Africa. If I re-let his room, I'll need to re-decorate and have the roof repaired.

'We could move into this room. It's much larger than yours.' Teresa stands in the doorway, in one of my white work shirts and nothing else.

'I'm going to run you home,' I say.

In the car Teresa says, 'I'm glad Rhys has gone. We'll have the place to ourselves. And no Shirley with her airs.'

'And knickers,' I say.

I drop Teresa outside her house.

'Pick me up next Friday,' she says.

'I don't know about next weekend,' I say. 'I may be stripping wallpaper.' But I do know.

I drive straight back to Rhys's new place. Outside the

front door there's one of those panels with names and buttons. Rhys has already put his and Shirley's surnames in the metal slot. I press the button and wait. I know he's in because his car is next to mine.

'It's me, Rhys,' I say.

'Mate, Shirley's cooked dinner. Candles, the works. New place. Come back in an hour.'

I sleepwalk around my flat and draw curtains, light the gas fire, turn on the television. There are lights on in Rhys's block but I don't know which is his. None of them look candlelit. I collect up the chair bits and put them out for the rubbish. I pile dishes in the sink, sweep the broken glass into my hand and drop it into an unbroken one, pour a brandy, sit in Rhys's chair.

I think about placing an ad in 'Room to Rent'. Ask Rhys to sift the applicants for me. Choose the girl he would've gone for. Maybe a girl like Shirley.

Vanishing Man

I evaporate from parties. Vanish like money. One minute I'm there, the next—

Which explains why I'm here, at hotel reception, eleven-o-clock at night, checking out. Telling the duty night manager the lie that I'm feeling unwell and need to go home and 'No, there was nothing wrong with the room.' In five minutes my car's navigation will be guiding me through the city streets to the motorway north.

I've fizzled out from a young age, even from my own birthday parties. The ones when, a month before, I'd make a list of the friends I wanted to invite, rub names out, pencil them back in.

'Aren't you going to invite some girls too? Wouldn't it be lovely to have some pretty girls in their party frocks?' Mum said.

Which is exactly what I wanted her to say, because there was Sarah Colman who showed me her knickers in the girl's toilet. I'd go to school with a handful of invites, like I was handing out medals.

After I'd puffed out the candles, when we'd played the games, I'd scut like a rabbit down its burrow. Whilst the others played hide and kiss in the garden, whilst Sarah Colman showed her knickers to another boy, I'd hop indoors. After a while someone came looking for me. I'd be lying on my bed reading *The Beano*.

I was the same at college. Those last-minute parties in grungy student digs. Bring your own booze. People carrying in bottles of wine, crates of beer, half bottles of vodka. There'd be weed and a novelty bottle of poppers. The guys in the kitchen necking the drink, coming on to the girls stirring the saucepan of curry. Couples in foreplay on the sofas, girls dancing in front of the TV, guys sitting on the stairs rolling joints, a girl crying in the bathroom because she's missed a period, some bloke in the corner with a stack of vinyl doing the DJ thing.

I'm brilliant at arrivals. I'd laugh through the hellos, shake hands with the males, kiss the females on the cheek, linger my lips on Sharon Spicer's, squeeze into the kitchen with my alcohol, start on the wine, drink it like water. Find Sharon. Attempt Jean-Paul Sartre conversation over the Bob Marley. I'd watch couples go upstairs to find bedrooms. Sharon would start dancing with her room-mate and two other guys. She's more alive with them. That's when I'd start to disappear. I'd become hazy, no-one could see me. Then silent, no-one could hear me. Then I'm outside, pacing home under the street-lights like a cat ready for breakfast.

At family parties I'd do my ghost act several times. Christmas parties at my ex-parents-in-law, I'd be the one to open the champagne and carve the turkey, the model son-in-law.

In bed with my ex-wife Sam, before dawn, even before the kids had opened their presents, I'd have said something like, 'We're only staying till four, aren't we?'

And Sam would've said something like, 'Don't be fucking stupid, it's Christmas Day.'

By Christmas pudding time we hadn't exchanged a word. That's when I'd start going to the toilet. I'd sit there with my head in my hands. When someone came upstairs, I'd flush and unlock, then sneak into the spare bedroom and close the door. I'd sit on the damp bedspread and read the religious shit on the framed prints. Then at four-o-clock I'd go downstairs and stare at Sam. She wouldn't meet my eye.

That's when I'd say, 'I think I've left the car window open,' and walk outside.

I'd sit in the car and move the windows up and down, take the dog for a walk, invent a sick child. Back indoors

I'd put my hand to their forehead, announce they had a temperature and pull out the whole family, with Sam saying, 'He feels alright to me.'

And then there was tonight. I knew Molly was going to be there. Molly knew I was coming. We said it would be fine.

'I'll kiss you on both cheeks. We're still friends for Christ's sake,' I texted.

'We'll be grown up about it,' she texted back.

I'd arrived after her. I made sure of that. I entered the function room which was all noise and welcome. I saw her from the corner of my eye. She was wearing a yellow dress. I laughed through the hellos, shook hands with the males, kissed the females on the cheek. People came over to me. I'm brilliant at arrivals. I sat next to the most attractive woman I could find, made sure we did lots of talking, made sure my head went close to hers. I drank too much wine. Drank it like water.

Where were we when our paths eventually crossed? Outside the toilets, at the bar, in the hot evening garden? I kissed her on both cheeks as promised, and we hugged for a second.

'Oh, hi,' we said, not a lot else. She'd have said more, been grown up about it, but I could feel myself vanishing.

My voice is the first to go. It moves inside my head, starts talking only to me. Then my ears absorb into my skull, sound closes down. I stop hearing people around me, conversations I'm part of go unheard. My limbs and torso are the next to go. People stop seeing me. I keep hold of my eyes till the final minute.

My eyes focused on Molly sat next to him, watched her touch his thigh. I returned her apologetic smile in my direction with my best 'I'm over it' smile in her direction.

Molly would've been the last one to see me.

Curdled Paint

The length of white painted wooden shelving had been a remnant from a bedroom redecoration, from a time when we cared what the bedrooms looked like. I'd cut the plank into six, nailed the pieces together into a cube and drilled a bird sized hole through the front.

I screwed the nesting-box to an ice-rimed alder tree, the frost clenching in the last light. In the corner of my eye I saw her watching through the bedroom window, but she didn't speak word of it, as though the box wasn't there, invisible.

That night I overheard her on the telephone to our escaped daughter.

'Your father's cobbled together a nesting-box but its painted white. Nothing will ever go near it. Homebuilding never was his strong suit.'

On the day the removal lorry arrived I took a last look inside that nesting-box. The cobwebbed space, a bird-sized version of the rooms in our emptying house; lifeless, loveless.

She was wrong. One year a pair of blue-tits did make a nest and fledge their young to the point when the chicks were preparing for flight. I remember watching crows plucking them out of the box by their tiny heads, swallowing them whole like oysters.

I yanked the nesting box off the tree and lobbed it into the skip, on top of other detritus from thirty years, including half empty pots of curdled paint, some of it white.

The Echoes

2035 AD. I never thought I'd make it this far. I never thought humanity would make it this far. I'm on a beach chair in the mouth of a cave. I've got a blanket over me and a bottle of whisky for company.

There's a spring tide tonight and the sea has already cut me off from the beach, but I'm not going anywhere. By sunrise the stars will be closer to Earth.

I've known the cave on this beach most of my life. The first time I stepped into it was on a family holiday in July 1969. We were staying in a fisherman's cottage that fronted onto a cobbled alleyway, us three kids all in one attic bedroom with a single skylight view of the moon.

On first sight of the cave we ran the length of the beach and yodelled and tumbled in the cool, deep sand. We made every echoing noise our mouths could shape, as every child before us had done, back to man's first footprint on this shore. From that day on we knew the cave as 'The Echoes'.

I remember the night during that holiday my father had climbed into the attic room and woken me.

'Come downstairs,' he said. 'History's being made.'

Chairs were pulled up close to a small television set, and there on the surface of the moon, a ladder waited for a space-boot to appear from 'The Eagle'. All the next day we played at being spacemen. The echoes in the cave amplified our rocket noises and staccato, astronaut voices.

We returned to the same beach and the unchanging Echoes every summer for the next five years. By then The Echoes had become our echoes, their rock walls inscribed with that period of our lives like stone-age drawings.

In the fruit machine arcade by the harbour, I met Pamela, both of us bored teenagers. I'd been standing behind her, watching her feed pennies into a one-armed bandit.

124

She had blond corkscrew hair with streaks of toffee brown. Her loose shirt exposed her bikini top, and under that I could see freckles falling into the white of her breasts. She smelt of vanilla ice-cream and seaweed.

'I'm out of money, freak,' she said. 'You want a go?'

I gave her one of my coins. 'Bring me luck.'

Three bells. Fifty one penny coins pulsed out of the machine. She'd untied the knot in her shirt-front and, holding up the hems, filled the cotton pouch. Before our winning streak ended Pamela took all the coppers to the woman in the booth and changed them for a fiver note.

'Let's walk to the beach,' she said, 'buy chips on the way.'

She'd taken my hand as we walked deep into The Echoes. We'd kissed until our lips were raw, tasting each other's salt and vinegar tongues. My hand shook as it made its way up her skirt and down her bikini briefs, feeling the velvet between her legs. The rising tide reached its hands of water into the cave and I was out of my depth.

I saw Pamela only once more on that holiday. She'd been with her family in the same beer-garden, pretending she hadn't seen me.

The next time I walked into 'The Echoes' was a decade later with my wife Sam. The town had changed in ten years. City types in 4x4s, yacht owners – Margaret Thatcher's Britain. When I led Sam into The Echoes, I found my initials I'd gouged into a rock as a kid. I told her about the night 'Eagle' had landed on the moon.

'I was too little to remember any of it,' she said and walked into the sunlight.

That evening we'd overdone the wine. A walk in the sea-shallows had sobered us up, but the alcohol had left another appetite. We made love up against The Echoes' walls whilst I thought of Pamela. Two months later Sam told me she was pregnant.

By the time our first grandchild was born I'd done well enough in business to buy a cottage in the town. Our family tree, in scratched initials on the walls of The Echoes, went back four generations.

For the last six months a spacecraft has been travelling towards Mars. Tonight, the landing module will touch down, a ladder will descend onto the red sand and my grand-daughter will be the first human to set foot on the Red Planet. I'll watch the satellite coverage on my tablet from this beach chair. She was chosen to name the module so it's 'The Echo' carrying mankind's faint reverberation across 140 million miles. These caves, these Echoes, have stayed solid and unchanging over the heads of my family for decades, and I'm as certain that 'The Echo' will bring my flesh and blood safely home.

By the time she returns to Earth I won't be here. My doctor showed me the lie of the land on the x-rays. At high tide, with this heavy swell, the churning water in these caves would be enough to drown a strong swimmer. With my legs and lungs, it will all be over quickly.

She's climbing down the ladder now, her voice echoing through space, splashing off every satellite dish, funnelling down every cable, washing over Earth. She has both feet on untrodden ground. Earth's cheers echo in the cave. The sun is rising in the Martian sky. The opalescence of sea-shell. The sound of waves.

Done Paris

The hotel was no more than a sign, a door off the street. Whilst we registered, girls with bare, scabby legs came and went from the rooms behind us. Crapulous men tapped on doors. You said it was ironic that we'd booked a hotel where the rooms were on hourly rent to the street whores.

'That's what I am now,' you said and dropped your wedding ring into your purse.

In the chill of our room the stained soft furnishings smelt of spilt sex, even more so just as soon as we closed the door. We ravaged each other, kerb-crawling talk, hard and trodden, until we were blooded, coal-eyed and sex-shocked, until the room was dark with the Parisian night, until our need for food and air was greater.

We showered together, stood in an embrace in the bathtub, but the hot water came in a trickle, not enough to cleanse even one. You sent me for towels that weren't filthy. The proprietor shrugged and said there were no more till morning.

We walked Montmartre until we found a boutique de salle de bains. They only stocked designer which cost more than the hotel room, but you said they're cheaper than paying for sex.

In the morning we queued for The Louvre. You wouldn't let me photograph you by the glass pyramid. You bought trinkets for your daughters. We marched through endless galleries, stopping to look at nothing, saying nothing. We peered over heads at the Mona Lisa, then left. We found a bistro where we were the only customers. I ordered oysters. You speared at a bowl of olives and we drank two bottles.

I wanted to find Montparnasse cemetery and the tombs of Sartre and Beckett. We asked a grey-haired couple for directions in classroom French. They were small and fragile as sparrows; they were holding hands. I showed them a map. You stroked their dog. They laughed at us. 'Pourquoi une cimetière? Vous êtes jeune, à Paris!' So we took the metro to the Eiffel Tower. When we arrived, you said you couldn't queue for anything else.

The bed linen hadn't been changed so we resumed on the towels. Whilst I slept you went out and booked yourself on an earlier flight home. Said you'd done Paris.

Boiler Man

The boiler man called me at two o'clock, as promised. 'It's the boiler man here,' he said. 'You're next on my list.'

'Can you remember where I am?' I asked.

'At the end of the track,' he said. I preferred to say 'lane'. The boiler man called things as he saw them.

I stood at my bedroom window waiting to catch a glimpse of his van. The December mist hadn't lifted, and the day hadn't got properly light. All the rooms in the house were cold, apart from the one where an electric heater clicked on a thermostat. Quiet pervaded, as though waiting for an arrival.

I wasn't sure if I recognised the van's blue and white livery when its sidelights came into view. When he stopped in my driveway and opened the driver's door, I recognised him. This man had kept my boiler running for over twenty years. I went downstairs, filled the kettle and opened the front door before he knocked. The boiler man hadn't changed since my last full service.

The leather trouser-belt around his waist resembled the tack of a plough-horse. I reckoned it to be as long as he was tall, and a quarter inch thick. His colossal stomach protruded from under his T-shirt like the boiler on a locomotive steam-engine; smooth and gleaming. The boiler man's stomach had never struck me as unhealthy – more a specimen of mechanical efficiency brought about through regular servicing. I felt ashamed that my broken down boiler hadn't been serviced in four years and that I hadn't kept in touch.

'I thought you were going to buy a new one,' he said, lifting the cover on my faulty appliance.

Four years ago, I said that I'd investigate a more modern version – something that would cut down my emissions, something with a leaner burn.

'I never got around to it. Now my wife and I are going to separate and sell the house, there isn't any point.'

When I told the boiler man about my marriage, it seemed he didn't need to be told what was wrong with my boiler. He stroked an internal pipe with an oily rag and inspected the rag for signs of abuse.

'Me and the wife's ruby this year,' he said, folding his rag.

'Amazing things, boilers' I said. 'What other machine could work so hard for twenty years without fail?'

The boiler man laid an altar cloth beneath my inlet valves. 'That's the thing, isn't it?' he said. 'People will replace their car but not their boiler.' With shortbread biscuits I steered us away from a deeper conversation.

When he left me to fetch new parts from his van, I watched from the kitchen window as he selected small boxes from compartmentalised, shallow drawers. Everything in the boiler man's life had its rightful place and usefulness. I left a cup of tea next to his cloth and took the opportunity to escape upstairs.

'Hello!' he called up the stairs for me. I remembered that he wouldn't be left alone. He was a large engine that ran smoothly when you stood next to it, admiring the wheels and pistons, but the minute you turned your back, it would begin to cough and splutter, and eventually stop working.

'Here's your problem,' he said, holding up a short, black plastic probe with a glass 'eye' on the tip. 'Your photocell. The glass eye has shattered.'

He held up a new one. 'For this boiler to work, it has to literally *see* the flame.'

He knelt before the boiler and rested his stomach on the tops of his legs. His head-torch shone like a halo into the bowels of the machine.

We both heard my wife moving about on the landing

upstairs. Before we agreed to separate, she would have come and said hello to the boiler man and the three of us would have talked about our children. He never left our home without knowing a little more about our offspring, and he wouldn't leave until we knew more about his. We talked our children up, but no children had succeeded like the boiler man's. His daughter was a senior policewoman who played cricket at county level. His son was in finance with a 'crazy package'. As my wife didn't come down, we skipped the subject.

'I once came out to a boiler in this village,' he said. 'I've never seen the like of.'

I moved closer, as he gave away trade secrets in hushed tones.

'It was nothing but a steel drum on a square of breeze-blocks. The old boy must have made it himself. You threw in a bucket of kerosene and a lighted match.'

'I think I know who you mean,' I told him. 'He flew bombers during the war.'

'He should have stuck to piloting.'

By now, my boiler was roaring. The radiators were warming up.

'My boiler can see again,' I said.

'Modern boilers run on blue flames,' he said. 'Exhaust-heat transfer.'

I shook my head in disbelief and followed him down to his van and watched him replace the unused parts in the compartmentalised drawers. There was room for everything in the boiler man's life; no messy, over-flowing, miscellaneous spaces.

'Give my regards to your wife,' he said.

'Thank you for everything you've done for us over the years,' I replied.

'You know where to find me,' he said.

The Twister

'I love funfairs,' Eva said. 'We have to go on something.'

Eva and Seb were walking the city walls, struggling to keep warm. Neither of them had gone prepared for the bitter wind that sliced off the Irish Sea and the chill damp of the north of England.

The fairground occupied the river meadows outside the high Roman walls that encircled the city. They could hear the loud, taped voices enticing people onto the rides. When they turned the corner on the castellated walkway, the multi-coloured, mechanised shapes came into view. A handful of parents with small children braved the weather among the striped roof of the dodgem cars, the gangling arms of 'The Octopus' and the hairpin bends of the sedate roller-coaster. Toddlers rode the sedate 'Cups and Saucers' or caught plastic ducks with a hook on the end of a pole. The teenagers would be waiting for nightfall, the lights and music. Not until after dark would the over-painted faces of screaming girls be seen on 'The Waltzers', nor the self-conscious young men arrive in their souped-up hatchbacks with thumping loud-speakers.

Eva took Seb's hand and pulled him down the stone steps to the meadow. He felt older than her, although he wasn't, not much. She had flashes of child-like excitement and looked younger; a foot shorter, slender limbs and junior sized feet in fashionable trainers, contrasting with his drab walking boots. She wore a brightly coloured pink bobble hat interwoven with tinselled wool that glittered against the grey sky. In the cafés where they stopped for hot drinks, she'd pull off the hat and shake loose her newly-dyed black hair, re-lipstick in a compact mirror and check for messages on her phone.

'I'm not going on any roller-coaster,' Seb said. 'They scare me to death.'

'We'll find a suitable ride for a couple of fifty-somethings,' Eva said, 'something we can get in and out of, unaided.'

They agreed on 'The Twister' because she said it was playing 'groovy music'. Eva stepped up from the sodden grass and slipped on the wet metal floor of the ride. She fell onto her side into the low slung, two-person carriage, catching her leg on the angular mechanism of the safety bar.

'Good start.' Seb laughed, and pulled her back into a sitting position. Then he saw she was crying.

The fall had torn her jeans at the thigh. There was blood on her hand where she covered the rip. Seb called the attendant and asked him to unlock the safety bar before the ride started. The attendant refunded their tickets without asking why, probably thinking they were just another middle-aged couple losing courage at the last minute.

'Why doesn't anything work for us?' she said. 'Why can't we even get on a fucking fairground ride and enjoy it?'

Seb led her limping to the outer perimeter of the fair where a few large trees stood in a loose circle.

'Go behind a tree and drop your jeans. Let me have a look,' he said. He took tissues from his pocket.

'I'm not stripping off in public.' Eva threw off his hand and limp-marched back towards the stone steps.

He caught up with her. 'Eva?'

'Fuck my life,' she said.

'It's a fairground ride, not your life.'

'Something else I can't manage without screwing up.'

They found a café and sat next to a radiator. Seb ordered tea while Eva went to the toilets. It was their last day and night together before she took the train back. Seb felt sure she'd been texting her husband. She was probably on her mobile to him from the privacy of the ladies.

'It's a deep cut,' Eva said. 'We need to find a chemist for a bandage, and somewhere to buy new jeans.'

Back at the weekend rent, Eva pulled off the ripped jeans and tried on the new pair.

'Great. They don't fucking suit me.'

'Then why did you buy them?'

'Because in the shop they did fucking suit me.' She ran up the stairs and slammed the bedroom door.

Seb found the sewing kit he'd seen in the bathroom cabinet. Whilst Eva dozed, he stitched together the rip. It wasn't perfect but it would hold, and her long sweater would cover his uneven attempt.

They went out for the last dinner of the weekend. She wore the jeans he'd repaired, the jeans he later unzipped as she lay flopped on the double bed. She wore them again the next morning for her train journey home.

'Sorry I was pathetic at the fair,' she said.

'One day we'll go to a giant funfair,' Seb said. 'I'll even go on a roller-coaster.'

'And I'll get on it without injuring myself.'

That same evening, Eva emailed Seb and told him it had to end. She said she couldn't rip her family apart. They kept in touch. She told him she wasn't happy and called herself a 'lost cause'. A year later, she sent a picture of herself wearing the repaired jeans. Said that she wore them constantly. That his handiwork had held things together.

Scream Without Sound

You rise from the horizontal on the sun-lounger and hold your unclasped bikini to your chest. Your skin glitters with oil. I can't see the expression on your face behind sunglasses, but I know you're thinking of something to say, something to split the over-ripe quiet. I continue with my slow lengths of the swimming pool, pushing off from the ends, gliding underwater until I can't hold my breath any longer.

You stand. 'Wine?' We break long silences with drink.

You walk indoors still holding the bikini top to your chest. I look at the white lines over your shoulders, the lines you've been working on. I've rubbed on oil whilst you lay on your front and turned pages of a paperback. The crisping sun has stifled everything; the children in neighbouring villas, the cars passing on the dirt track to the beach, the breeze that ripples through the fig leaves and over the sapphire water. You've never exposed your breasts to me, except under the sheets, under me.

Last night I said, 'I've never seen you naked out of bed.'

'Why would you want to?'

'Isn't that what couples do?'

'Is it? I've never thought of us as a "couple".'

I glide to the side of the pool with my face underwater, hold my breath, wait for you, observe my feet on the bottom of the pool. I imagine what it would be like to take in lungfuls of water, not to breath until my vision turns to black, to scream without sound. I spring up, gasping, rest my forearms on the scorching tiles, splash water out of the pool to cool the surface. Then you are there, holding a bottle and two glasses against your bare white breasts. A nipple is pressed like a mouth against the wineglass I'm about to drink from.

On my back, I push off and float towards the opposite side. When my outstretched fingers touch, I watch you sit and swing your legs into the water, then pour. I bob my head in and out. I can see the blurred outlines of your knees from under the surface. I push off again, glide and rise between them. You hand me a glass. I swivel, turn my back to you and look over to the orange grove on the other side of the rough concrete wall.

'Left it late for an all over tan.'

You don't answer me. You rise to your feet and drop your bikini bottoms next to the bottle. You walk into my vision at the top of the pool and dive in. Your shape comes towards me and rises to my lips.

'There, happy now?' you say. You start pulling at my shorts. 'Is this what couples do?'

I snatch away your hand and side-step back underwater. I swim to the pool ladder and climb out.

I watch you reach for your things and dress under cover of the water. I strip and wait in the shuttered darkness of the bedroom.

Rose Petals on the Bed

Fenella spins on the dance floor like the music box fairy on her dressing table back home. Round and round she goes, on one fat leg then the other. The wide, gauzy underskirts of her wedding dress brush over the pin pricks of ever changing coloured lights in the floor, so one minute her bottom half is seashell pink and the next, an azure blue. There's a handful of other people in the nightclub and they're all watching her, amused and entranced by her unselfconscious gyrations.

This is the third time the DJ has played *I Think I Want to marry You*, and each time the singer sings the words 'Marry You' Fenella points with both index fingers at her new husband Barry, and he points back. 'MARRY YOU!' They laugh each time as if the thought was newly minted. Barry has modernised his baldness with an all-over shave. His scalp and white waistcoat change colour in sync with his wife's underskirts. She'd rubbed some of her tanning cream onto his bald head before the marriage ceremony and he'd rubbed some over her expansive chest, above and below the neckline of her dress.

Barry had been her boss at Alpha Auto Clutch and Brakes before their relationship went public, then she'd been asked to resign. It was Barry who'd suggested they got married on a cruise ship. Barry had shown her the brochure. Beneath the title 'Enjoy a Day of Love, Laughter and Celebration' was a picture of a suntanned couple under an awning emblazoned with the name of cruise company, tropical flowers in hollowed out pineapples and the sea glittering in the background. When Fenella had read 'Includes a six inch, iced celebration cake and rose petals on the bed' she was sold. Her three-year old son was left at her sisters for the week and Barry had left his ex-wife and two boys pretty much everything he'd got.

There's one other person on the dance floor with Fenella and Barry. Fenella's mother, in the same dress she's worn to every *do* she's ever been to, sways alongside her daughter and new son-in-law, taking photos of them with her mobile phone. There hadn't been any other guests at the ceremony other than Fenella's mother, the Captain who officiated in his white uniform and the young female Head of Events called Chelsea. Chelsea had taken the complimentary photograph with Fenella piped in between the Captain and Barry, like whipped cream.

I Think I Want to marry You comes to an end. Fenella and Barry point at each other one last time, laugh, kiss, then Barry leaves the dance floor to order more drinks. A middle aged drunk on a barstool says that the next round is on him and orders champagne. Four women sat at a low table in the shadows giggle as they watch Fenella and her stiff-jointed mother attempt to dance to rap music. One of the women whispers a comment about Fenella's bulging legs wrapped around Barry's bottom in the honeymoon cabin.

'Like chicken sausages on a boiled quail's egg,' and they all shriek.

The drunk follows Barry back onto the dance floor with the bottle and four glasses intertwined in his fingers. Barry makes the introductions to Fenella and her mother. The drunk kisses both women on the back of their hands, pours the champagne and toasts, 'The happy couple.' He clinks glasses with Fenella's mother – the newlyweds are away, hugging each other close in a slow dance.

Back in their economy cabin, with no balcony or porthole, Fenella lays semi-comatose on the bed. Barry plucks off her shoes and rolls down her damp stockings and plus-size French knickers. Fenella had promised they'd fuck whilst she still had her dress on. Barry unties his bow tie and checks his phone. There's a text from his kids

138

wishing him a Happy Wedding. Through prickly eyes he composes a reply with an image of the ship's funnels, then presses delete.

Fenella has her head turned on the pillow looking at the complimentary framed wedding photo. She thinks if they'd been married at home her son could have been a pageboy in his Spiderman suit. She feels like she's going to throw up. They've eaten the whole wedding cake and drained God knows how many bottles of champagne with the drunk until he fell over and Barry had to slop him into a chair. The ship is lolling from side to side on the sea swell and Fenella isn't sure she can make it to the toilet.

Further down the corridor of cabin doors Fenella's mother slots in her key card. The drunk, a divorced greengrocer from Colwyn Bay, follows her in with both hands on her backside. With one hand Barry picks rose petals off Fenella's back as she pukes into the toilet on all fours, her French knickers still wrapped around one ankle. With the other hand he texts his ex-wife to ask what days next week he's having the boys.

The Night Fisher

Hart walks alone through the small seaside town, along the
narrow road towards the rocks. In one hand he carries an
old fishing rod. The tip of the rod, bent down with lead
weights, jounces up and down in time with his footsteps. In
his other hand he carries a tackle box that rattles with spare
hooks, spinners, floats, spools, other ephemera never
unpacked.

Sitting outside at pub tables, under umbrellas
advertising cider, holiday-makers take their eyes off dinner
menus and watch his passing. They survey his gardening
boots, his unfashionable coat, the gathering gloom.

Hart sees them thinking, *'Night fisher. Local. He'll
catch.'*

Hart doesn't live anywhere near the coast. He hasn't
fished since they stayed in the same seaside town, twenty
years ago. Their sons were with them then, eager with their
new rods and brightly coloured buckets. After thirty
minutes of nothing the boys would leave their rods on the
rocks, throw stones into the swell or disembowel the bait
with penknives. Their mother would fetch them for bath
and bedtime.

'Any luck?' she'd ask.

They'd show her a crab they'd picked out of the rock
pools.

'After all that money,' she'd say.

As a boy, when he'd fished with his father, Hart had
always caught. His mother sat with them, poured soup
from a thermos and handed out sandwiches. Bedtimes
were later then, and baths were once a week. In the
morning his father would gut the fish over the sink and his
mother would fry them for breakfast. They'd wipe their
plates with sliced bread, wash it down with cups of milky

tea then, at low tide, dig fresh lugworm from the harbour mud.

Hart walks past fishermen's cottages converted into holiday lets. Crew-cut lawns slope down to the water, wetsuits drip from clotheslines. Larger detached houses with bottles of sparkling wine on teak garden furniture. Yacht tenders rock alongside private moorings. The road peters out into a grassy track. A wooden signpost points to the coastal path. As he walks, he watches a crab boat leave the harbour on the flood tide. Fishermen in oilskin trousers lean on the gunwales. A small passenger ferry with white bunting chatters over to the opposite side.

There's just one other fisherman on the rocks. The usual detritus around his feet. Bloody bait on a newspaper, rusty knife, tin of tobacco, plastic carrier bag with the arc of dead fish.

Hart and the other fisherman nod to each other. 'Anything happening?'

'Couple of mackerel. Not a lot.'

Hart hopes that will be the end of the conversation until one of them catches, or leaves.

He'd rigged the tackle earlier, out on the small sunlit patio of the cottage they'd rented. Like setting a trap or mending a clock. Everything in its careful place and correct order. Pinhead knots. Balanced weights. The glint of metal, fine as cotton.

'You're not going fishing again?' his wife asked. 'That's every night of the holiday.'

'You could always come. Keep me company,' Hart said.

'It's not as if you ever catch anything,' she said, and went back into the cottage.

Hart finds his spot on the rocks, puts down his tackle

box, unclips the lid. The shelves expand outwards and upwards like stairs. At the bottom of the box, a vacuum-packed plastic envelope of sand-eels. She'd made him wrap the sand-eels in two layers of newspaper before he'd put them in the fridge.

'Stinks the place out otherwise,' she said.

Hart slits open the plastic with his penknife and takes out a single sand-eel, silver and sharp as the blade. He threads the hook through the eye socket and out through the mouth, cuts it in half, keeps the tail end for later. The float, weights and hook swarm through the early evening sky. The float lies on the water for a second as the weights take up the slack, then stands up straight, ducking and weaving on the tide.

Across the estuary the larger town reflects light and sound over the myriad of craft at anchor. People dawdle on the streets, sit at outdoor restaurant tables. Children swing on the harbour railings, pull crabs from the weedy shallows on lines baited with bacon. On the rocks, the only sound is from the rising water that sucks and swells into every nook.

The sulphur yellow top of Hart's float jerks slightly under, then up. His eye is already attuned to the float's small differences in downward movement between wave and fish. He puts both hands onto the rod handle, holds his breath. The tendons in his wrists wait for the instinct to snap. The float goes under. He flicks up, feels the opposing underwater tug and twist.

'On one?' The soft voice of the other fisherman.

'Something.' Hart tries to keep his voice low, unsurprised.

Hart reels in. Flashes of silver and gold, imperfections in the black sea. He lifts his treasure onto the rocks and admires the fish in both hands. Then he smacks its head on the rock. Hard. Quick. Hart had wanted to teach this to his own sons.

'Is that breakfast taken care of?' He starts at the voice. His wife descends from the path, onto the rocks.

She shares food she's brought in a carrier bag and pours hot drinks from a thermos.

'Tide's turned. I'll stop now,' he says.

They sit shoulder to shoulder on the rocks and watch the night haul its catch.

Blood and Electricity

A collection of short stories by Steven John

Grateful acknowledgement is made to the following written competitions, anthologies and journals in which previous versions of these stories first appeared:

The Beautiful Couple (2022) – Anti heroin Chic

Bluebells, Cockle Shells (2021) – Frigg Magazine

Blueberry Muffins (2018) – The Cabinet of Heed

Boiler Man (2021) – Frigg Magazine

A Brief History of Time in our House (2018) – Ad Hoc Fiction

Canada (2019) – The Blake-Jones Review

Canoe (2017) – Reflex Fiction

Chameleons (2020) – Pithead Chapel

Curdled Paint (2019) – Crepe & Penn

The Dead Dog Tree (2019) – New Flash Fiction Review

Done Paris (2019) – Spelk

A Gathering of Driftwood (2018), *A Girl Like Shirley* (2019), *The Lake* (2019), *Profile Pictures* (2022), *Rose Petals on the Bed* (2019), *Sea Loch* (2019), *Under the Paint* (2018) – Fictive Dream

Giants (2019) – Bending Genres

Holly's Party (2019) – Ellipsis Zine

The Leopard Cup (2020) – Virtual Zine

Nap of The Cloth (2020) – National Flash Fiction Day

The Night Fisher (2018) – Riggwelter

Scream Without Sound (2019) – Ghost Parachute

Sculpted Bones (2016), *Fashion in Men's Footwear* (2018) – Stroud Short Stories Volume 2, edited by John Holland

Burning the Stubble (2019), *Puffballs* (2020), *The Orange Tree* (2022) – Stroud Short Stories Volume 3, edited by John Holland

The Twister (2021) – Frigg Magazine

Vanishing Man (2019) – Lunate Fiction

About the Author

Since he started writing in 2015, Steven John's award-winning short fiction and poetry have appeared in online magazines, printed anthologies, and in live on-stage events including The Cheltenham Literary Festival and Stroud Short Stories. Steven served as International Fiction Editor for the US publication *Best Microfiction*, Special Features and Senior Fiction Editor on the long-established *New Flash Fiction Review*, and then as Joint Founding and Managing Editor on *The Phare* – an online showcase of short fiction, poetry, and creative non-fiction.

Steven now works as a part-time Lecturer in Creative and Critical Writing at the University of Gloucestershire, supervising Post Graduate students during their dissertation process. He also runs creative writing workshops in his local community.

Steven says he lives 'perilously close' to the banks of the River Severn in North Gloucestershire and that sometimes the walls of his house *are* the banks of the River Severn. He is currently working on a novella-in-flash and a second collection of short stories. When he's not teaching, writing, or erecting his flood defences, Steven enjoys being with his children and grandchildren, cooking elaborate meals, and dreaming of being a celebrity chef.

www.stevenjohnwriter.com

Like to Read More Work Like This?

Then sign up to our mailing list and download our free collection of short stories, *Magnetism*. Sign up now to receive this free e-book and also to find out about all of our new publications and offers.

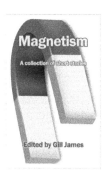

Sign up here:
  http://eepurl.com/gbpdVz

Please Leave a Review

Reviews are so important to writers. Please take the time to review this book. A couple of lines is fine.

Reviews help the book to become more visible to buyers. Retailers will promote books with multiple reviews.

This in turn helps us to sell more books... And then we can afford to publish more books like this one.

Leaving a review is very easy.

Go to https://amzn.to/4f5Dj7q, scroll down the left-hand side of the Amazon page and click on the 'Write a customer review' button.

Other Publications by Bridge House

The Story Weaver
by Sally Zigmond

Story-telling has often been associated with weaving and spinning. All is craft, cleverness and magic.

Here indeed we have a colourful mix of beautifully crafted stories. Some are sad and others bring us hope. There are tensions in relationships, fear of the unknown coupled with surprising empathy, and accidents of birth. Death wishes are reversed, sometimes but not always, and so are lives in other realties. People's stories intersect as they wait for a bus. An old cello causes havoc. A church clock always strikes twice… or does it? Match-making goes wrong until it goes right. And so much more.

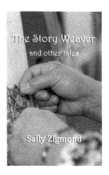

'A wonderful collection of interesting tales. A real mixture that will delight all readers.' *(Amazon)*

Order from Amazon:

Paperback: ISBN 978-1-914199-54-7
eBook: ISBN 978-1-914199-55-4

The Adventures of Iris and Zach
by I.L. Green

Iris and Zach have an uneasy but intriguing run.

A vast patchwork landscape of life is displayed through stories relating both the wonder and absurdity we all recognize. With a focus on mental health, these stories take the reader from incarceration to freedom, fear to comfort. There are celebrations of life and poetic lows. The Yin and Yang aspects of life are recognized in new and deliberate examples that instil thoughtfulness and occasionally a smile.

Order from Amazon:

Paperback: ISBN 978-1-914199-34-9
eBook: ISBN 978-1-914199-35-6

Weird Science
by Doug Hawley

Who would have thought it?

An abominable snowman speaks, dreams so good you'll never want to wake up, metaphysical questions, a cat with telepathy, a magical stream in USA's Northwest, and an unexpected invasion from the far north of Canada.

You will find all this and more in one book of Weird Science.

Order from Amazon:

Paperback: ISBN 978-1-914199-40-0
eBook: ISBN 978-1-914199-41-7

9 781914 199806